Sparkling Stilettos

A SPARKLING NOVEL

JESS WRIGHT

Sparkling Stilettos
ISBN # 978-1-78430-570-3

Interior text design by Claire Siemaszkiewicz
Totally Bound Publishing

Published in 2015 by Totally Bound Publishing, Newland House, The Point, Weaver Road, Lincoln, LN6 3QN, United Kingdom.

Totally Bound Publishing is a subsidiary of Totally Entwined Group Limited.

SPARKLING STILETTOS

Dedication

Dedicated to my family, who are my world.

1

Megan

"Oh my goodness, darling, you look fabulous. Utterly…totally…bloody fabulous."

Megan held her full champagne flute to Brendon's and they chinked rims, the sound tinkling around the plush West London hotel room.

"Thank you," she said then hesitated with the glass by her lips. She stared in the mirror at her unfamiliar bridal reflection. With her dark hair piled high, her makeup natural and long, dangling silver earrings, she hardly recognised herself. "But do you think it's maybe a bit over the top, you know, with the tiara?"

"No, no, not at all," Brendon said, shoving his hand on his waist and jutting out his left hip. "You, my beauty, are a princess, so of course you should be wearing a bejewelled crown." He tutted and tapped the base of her stem. "Sup, sup, it's your wedding day, champers needs to be drunk from dawn till dusk."

"Yes, but not too much," Georgie said with a smile but also a hint of sternness in her tone. "We don't want you sloshed as you walk down the aisle, Megan. You've got towering heels to keep control of. Beautiful, bespoke heels yes, I agree, but still, they're high even for you."

Megan took a deep breath and curled her toes into the soft beige carpet—her feet were a little cold even though the room was warm. In one hour she would be wearing the stunning new heels she'd designed and walking down the aisle to marry Dylan Dunkin-Buckshaw—yes, she would be Mrs Megan Rose Dunkin-Buckshaw and damn proud to be.

She could live with the name. Of course she could. She'd be sad to say goodbye to Winter, though, because Megan Rose Winter had a nice ring to it. But she'd used the name Winter to set up her beloved shoe design business a few years before, so if she looked at it like that, she wasn't really giving up her name. She'd still have it, and still use it on a daily basis. The only difference would be that her driving licence and bank account would say Dunkin-Buckshaw. But what did that matter? Who ever saw a person's licence or bank account? Well, Dylan would see her bank account now. He'd said they'd pool their cash once married—apparently that was what couples did after tying the knot.

"Are you sure you're not going for the red?" Brendon held up her scarlet MAC lipstick. It was her favourite, the only one she wore. But today she'd decided not to. Today she was going for nude gloss.

"No." She shook her head. "Dylan doesn't really like it. He says it's..." She paused, remembering the conversation.

"What?" Georgie fussed with a tendril of Megan's hair that had escaped. "What does he say?"

"Yes, tell us?" Brendon added with a frown. "I'm curious now."

"He thinks it's a bit tarty."

Georgie gasped and shook her head. "No!"

Brendon slapped his hand over his mouth and widened his eyes.

"He said that?" Georgie asked. "He actually, really and truly said that?"

Megan shrugged. It was no big deal. He was entitled to have an opinion.

"But you've worn that shade for years." Brendon tutted. "It's so…you. It's your signature lippy."

"And it suits you so well, highlights the pretty shape of your mouth," Georgie added.

"Thank you, but it's just for today."

"Are you sure?" Brendon asked. "Because if you never wear it again I'll be heartbroken. In fact, I may as well just lie down here right now and die." He gestured to the four-poster bed then made a show of falling back onto it. He threw his arms over his face. "Oh, goodbye to the scarlet lips that we know and love. How can I go on?"

"Don't be so dramatic, it's only lipstick." Megan laughed. "Come on. Help me with the dress."

Georgie glanced at her iPhone. "Yes, you should get dressed. Time is ticking away. The bells will soon be ringing."

Megan stood. Her stomach was heavy even though she hadn't been able to eat that morning. Nerves, most likely. This was, after all, the biggest day of her life—or so she'd been told. If she wasn't nervous there'd be something wrong with her, right? If there were no butterflies swarming she'd be abnormal. Every bride had this sensation, she'd read about it, seen it in movies.

"How does this feel?" Georgie asked, adjusting the ties on the back of the white basque Megan wore. "Too tight?"

"No it's fine. It kind of feels like it's holding me together." Megan huffed at her silliness but it was the truth. With all the emotions rolling about inside her—apprehension, excitement, awestruck—the basque was like wearing a hug. It was comforting and made her feel secure.

"Your new husband will love that later," Brendon said, crawling off the bed and nodding approvingly. His gaze took in Megan standing in her sexy underwear. "My, my, if I wasn't into men, my sweetpea, I'd do you."

"Well thanks, I think." Megan giggled and reached for a pack of unopened white stockings.

"Who are you kidding, Brendon?" Georgie said, before picking up her champagne and taking a sip. "I shouldn't think you've got the energy for any of that after last weekend."

"Last weekend was a business trip." Brendon scowled.

"Hah, business, yes, if you're in the business." Georgie rolled her eyes. "Everyone knows that you and Timothy Hung-like-a-Donkey Curtis weren't interested in checking out that hotel in Brighton for a possible gig, you were just on a shagathon trip."

"Well, I take great offence to that, Georgie Porgy Pudding and Pie, because actually that's exactly what we did. Prada is looking at holding a launch party there for their new line of summer purses"

"Yes, we'll believe it when we see it." Georgie laughed and set down her glass.

Normally Megan's ears would have pricked at the mention of Prada summer purses—she loved purses for all seasons and all occasions—but not today.

"You want me to do that, Megan?"

"No, I can manage." The wrapper on the stocking box was proving tricky and her hands were a little shaky.

"Here." Georgie took the package and deftly opened it.

"Thanks." Megan smiled. She was so happy that her two best friends were with her today. She couldn't have done it without them. They were her rocks, her pillars of support, her port in a storm. They'd met over five years ago at a mutual friend's party, all newly single and all wanting to have some fun. Before long they'd been partying hard, but also kicking back and putting the world to rights together. Now they spoke or dropped in on each other most days, did lunch or met for cocktails every week, and tried to get away at least once each summer to worship the sun on some tropical beach.

"Don't look so worried," Georgie said with a slight frown.

"Yeah, are you okay?" Brendon asked.

"I'm fine, absolutely fine." Megan took a deep breath. "Come on, let's get this show on the road." She gathered the first stocking and carefully fed her right foot into it then pulled it up to her thigh. She repeated the action with her left and smoothed the lace holdup trims to ensure there were no creases.

"Ah, ah, one more thing before the dress." Georgie dipped into her handbag. "Here."

"A garter?" Megan queried. "Really? Isn't that kind of old-fashioned?"

"Of course it's old-fashioned, it's traditional." Brendon nodded seriously. "Something old, something new, something borrowed, something blue."

"Yes, you have to wear one. It would be bad luck otherwise." Georgie sank to her knees at Megan's feet, garter held into a wide 'O'. She smiled up at Megan. "The tiara is old, the dress is new and this is something borrowed and..." She twisted the garter to show off a tiny blue bow. "Is also blue."

"Oh, okay." Megan giggled at how serious her friends were taking this tradition. What was going to happen if she didn't have something old, new, borrowed and blue? It would hardly spoil the day or curse their marriage for all of time.

Would it?

Georgie slipped the garter up Megan's leg to her thigh.

Megan stroked her finger over the delicate white trim. It was very pretty and no doubt Dylan would enjoy removing it when they reached the bridal suite—possibly with his teeth.

"This dress is to die for," Brendon said, holding up Megan's voluminous gown. "All this taffeta, it's enough to sink a battleship."

"Yes, I'll certainly have to navigate carefully through doorways today," Megan said then took a sip of champagne. She set the glass aside. "Come on then, help me into the monster." She laughed.

Georgie didn't laugh with her, instead she sighed and clasped her hands under her chin.

"You okay, Georgie?" Megan asked.

"Yes, of course. I'm just so happy for you and that this day has finally come. We've all talked for years about who would be first to get hitched and now it's happening."

Megan reached for her hand and squeezed. "It will happen for you and Tom soon, I'm sure it will."

Georgie and Tom had been together for over a year and things were getting serious. They'd skied at Christmas, met the parents and both had a drawer at each other's apartment for spare clothes and toiletries—surely a sign of true commitment.

Megan shrugged. "Maybe, maybe not, but it doesn't matter today. Today is all about you and Dylan."

"Who is likely to be arriving at church with his best man as we speak," Brendon said, before clicking his tongue on the roof of his mouth. "There is an expectant groom waiting, so chop, chop ladies. Enough of this chatter, you two could talk for England."

"And you couldn't?" Georgie grinned.

It took both her friends to assist Megan into her dress. Luckily she could step into it, which meant her hair and makeup weren't in danger, but still, the sheer amount of material created quite a challenge.

Brendon fussed over the many hems, straightening the layers and fluffing it out so the periphery was even bigger. Georgie fiddled with the top, drawing up the side zipper and puffing the cupped silk sleeves.

"It's so beautiful," Georgie said wistfully.

"And so virginal," Brendon said, then cackled. "Except we know that's not true."

Megan skimmed her palms over the tight material at her waist then over her hips. Her hands became lost in the meringue nest of taffeta. "I've had some fun but I have standards." She rolled her eyes. "But not as much fun as you, Brendon."

"Yeah, well, I've not finished having fun yet," he said, standing. "There's many more fish out there for me to reel in and have my wicked way with."

"But don't you want to find *the one*?" Georgie asked, helping herself to a squirt of Megan's perfume.

"Yes of course, but not for a while. I've still got things I want to do, places to go, people to meet. I'm not ready to commit to one person, and besides, I wouldn't know if it was the right person anyway."

"What do you mean?" Megan asked, taking her perfume from Georgie and spritzing it over her neck and onto her wrists.

"Well, I don't know how you do it." He looked between them. "How you can be so sure you've met your soulmate? The man you're meant to be with for all of time. Go to bed with each night and wake up each morning next to."

"You'll just know," Georgie said.

"But how?" Brendon held up his palms. "How? Enlighten me."

"When you count the hours till you're going to see them again," Georgie said. "Think of them when planning what to eat that night so you know they'll enjoy it. Watch boring old war documentaries because that's their thing and not mind in the least because you're snuggled up on the sofa next to them. That's how you know."

Megan studied her friend. Georgie lit up when she talked of Tom. He'd captured her heart in a way no other man had. She'd never seen her so happy, so full of life—even the asthma that had always plagued her seemed to have settled. It was as if Tom's presence in her life was a soothing energy, a balm for her nerves. Megan hoped Tom would pop the question soon. It would feel so right to see Georgie in an elegant white gown walking down the aisle.

The door to the hotel room opened. Megan's mother, Iris, walked in carrying Gucci, who barked and wriggled as soon as he saw Brendon.

"Baby boy," Brendon said, rushing to pluck his tiny Pomeranian from Iris' arms. Gucci's little pink tongue rushed out to lick his master's chin and his tail waggled to a rapid tempo.

"Oh, Rose, my beautiful English Rose," Iris said, halting in her tracks as soon as she saw Megan. Her eyes misted and she pressed her lips together.

"Mum, you promised not to cry," Megan said, knowing that her mother would. She only ever called her Rose when she was feeling sentimental, and since she'd moved to Australia three years ago, she was more sentimental than ever when the family got together.

"I can't help it," Iris said. "My little girl all grown up and getting married."

"Yes, it seems that way." Megan smiled and fluffed the tulle on her dress. "What do you think?"

"I think you look beautiful. Dylan is lucky to have you. Very lucky indeed."

"Here, here to that." Georgie nodded.

"Abso-bloody-lutely," Brendon said, slipping a tiny doggie tuxedo over Gucci's head. It had a small bow tie beneath the chin, an embroidered waistcoat and tails that hung either side of Gucci's…tail.

Megan walked over to her mother and, stretching over the width of the dress, hugged her.

"No, no, please don't let me mess you up," Iris said, sniffing delicately.

"You won't mess me up, Mum, it's all fine." Megan placed a soft kiss on her mother's cheek. She smelt of lavender, as usual, and her skin was soft as satin.

"Oh, but I might." Iris gave Megan a frantic squeeze then pulled away. "And you look so perfect. It all looks so perfect." She gestured at the door. "I've checked the cake and it's fabulous, exactly how Dylan wanted, a cascade of sparkling roses from the top tier to the base. The flowers are beautiful too, at the entrance to the reception room. The sweetest shade of baby pink and more gypsophila than you could shake a stick at."

"Good, that's good," Brendon said. "Flowers and cake are important."

"Where's Olivia?" Megan asked, wondering where her sister was. Olivia was her third bridesmaid.

"She's downstairs, with your father."

"I bet she looks beautiful." Megan adored how her bridesmaid dress complimented her sister's colouring. "What about Dad? Is he okay?" Megan asked, reaching for a tissue. She passed it to her mother, who instantly started checking her mascara hadn't run.

"He's fine with your sister, she's keeping an eye on him. She's good like that. You know, at calming him when he gets anxious."

"Yes, Olivia's great with him. But why's he anxious?" Megan hated seeing her father nervous. He was an all-round great guy, her rock, and as she'd grown from child to adult their relationship had only deepened. She loved him with all her heart.

"He's about to give away his eldest daughter, of course he's anxious. He's not so keen on giving away something so precious to him." Iris laughed but it held a note of tension. "And you most certainly are precious to him, Rose."

"Maybe he should look at it like he's gaining a son rather than giving away a daughter," Brendon said, ruffling Gucci's forehead so his fudge-coloured curls stood upright.

"I suppose," Iris said, sucking in a deep breath. "Yes, maybe that's how to look at it."

Megan studied her. She looked worried. Likely because Dad was stressed, even though he needn't be, he only had to walk a few steps down the aisle—not that she wouldn't be glad of his arm. Georgie was right, those heels, while stunning and one of her best designs yet, were hard to negotiate.

"Can you do me up?" Georgie asked, stepping in front of Megan. She'd pulled on her baby pink bridesmaid dress but the back zip was awkward for her to reach.

Megan slid it up. Georgie's hourglass frame suited the figure-hugging style perfectly and reminded her of a Marilyn Monroe photograph she'd seen once. Not least because Georgie's bubbles of blonde hair had just been cropped to jaw-length.

"Oh, Georgie," Iris said, "that dress is amazing on you. The colour is gorgeous with your skin tone and your eyes…simply stunning."

"Thank you," she said, turning back to Iris. "I'm glad Megan didn't pick lime green, I couldn't have pulled that off."

"I bet you could have worked lime green perfectly well." Megan laughed, though it was slightly forced because underneath Georgie's smile she knew there was a hint of longing. She wanted what Megan was about to have, a husband. But it would come soon, she was sure of it. Tom would eventually get around to it and bag the best thing that had ever happened to him.

"What about us?" Brendon said, striding in front of the mirror.

Gucci ran around his ankles, yapping as usual and hoping to be picked up again.

"How do we look?"

"Like the handsomest, gayest bridesmaid ever," Georgie said then laughed.

Megan reached to tickle Gucci beneath his chin but he wouldn't stay still for long enough, and besides, she could hardly reach him because of the dress. "And the handsomest doggie bridesmaid ever."

"Yes, I think we'll do." Brendon snapped down the pink satin waistcoat he wore beneath his morning suit. He then straightened the rose buttonhole. He looked good and he knew it. He even twirled around to check out his bum in the neat black trousers he wore, flicking up the tails of his morning coat to be sure.

"But we really should get going," Georgie said, again worrying about the time. "I know it's only a few minutes to the church from here but still, it's only ten minutes until the ceremony is due to start."

"Really?" Megan glanced at the clock that sat on the bedside table. Georgie was right. It was time to go.

It was time to go and get married.

And become Mrs Dunkin-Buckshaw.

Forever.

Her stomach clenched, the corset seeming to pull her muscles in even more.

Mr and Mrs Dylan Dunkin-Buckshaw.

The nerve endings in her scalp and at the base of her neck tingled. Maybe she should take Brendon's advice to her mother and look at it as not losing her name but gaining another family. There was Dylan's brother, his father and of course, his mother.

His mother. Rita. Who had been so excited about the wedding that Megan had actually stopped taking her calls in the final stages of preparation—not to be cruel, it was just too much. Her squeaky voice and over enthusiasm was draining, and Megan needed some energy left for the big day.

She'd called her yesterday, though, had bitten the bullet and picked up the phone. As she'd expected, it had been an hour of hysteria that had ranged from wild excitement to desperate despair because the napkins weren't the right shade of baby pink—how many shades of baby pink could there be?

"You okay, sweetpea?" Brendon took Megan's left hand.

"Yes, I think so." She looked at her hand in his. Her ring finger was bare, not even an indent. She'd hardly worn her engagement ring over the last six months, she'd been too worried about it getting wrecked at work with the glue she used on her designs. Now the ring was transferred to her right hand so that the new wedding band could be easily slipped on.

"You sure?" Georgie asked.

Megan pulled in as deep a breath as she could with the corset on. Her breasts pushed against the bones and she was aware of her heart thumping faster than normal.

"What is it?" Brendon asked.

"Nothing, nothing at all. I'm fine." Megan forced her mouth to turn up at the corners. "Really, let's get this show on the road."

"I'll see you there," her mother said. "Georgie and Brendon are very capable bridesmaids."

"And Gucci," Brendon added.

"And Gucci." Iris reached down and patted Gucci on the head. He licked her hand then ran excitedly in a circle.

"Yep, see you there, Mum," Megan said.

And next time we speak I'll be married.

"If I don't get the chance to say this to you later, Rose," her mother said, "know that I only ever want what is best for you. You make me so proud in everything you do, not least because you're a woman who knows what you want and you're not afraid to take it."

Megan felt her eyes tingle and her throat thicken. Tears were threatening.

A woman who knows what she wants and takes it.

2

"Go," Brendon said to Iris. "Go, go. We have to get this party started and get this beautiful bride blushing." He set a kiss on Iris' cheek then opened the door.

Iris turned and walked out, her heels sinking into the deep carpet. She tilted her chin and set her shoulders down as though gathering her resolve.

Brendon scooped up Gucci when he tried to follow and slotted his tiny body under his arm. He kept the door open.

"Shoes," Georgie said, setting the sparkling bridal sandals that Megan had designed on the floor.

"Oh, yes, thank you," Megan said, holding up her dress then slipping them on. They felt amazing, made to measure, and the insoles were cushioned so that the balls of her feet wouldn't ache even by the end of the day. If she wasn't wearing her lipstick, at least she had on her signature heels. Heels that made her feel taller, lighter, brighter and made her heart sing.

"Come on, come on." Brendon waved his arm dramatically. "You are going to be late for your own damn party."

"A bride is traditionally late," Megan said, glancing around the room. It was a nice suite. The walls were painted a warm, cosy burgundy and the dark wooden furniture was solid and sturdy, likely antique too. The bed looked inviting, she was tired, sleep had been hard to find the night before.

"Megan?" Georgie rested her hand on Megan's back.

"Let's do this," Megan said, determination suddenly flooding her. Brendon was right. She couldn't be any later than she already was. A whole congregation awaited her. Family and friends. Some—like her parents and sister—had travelled halfway around the world to share her and Dylan's special day.

Dylan was waiting for her too. He'd be worried—he'd fidget, his eyes would narrow the way they did when he was anxious and he'd speak to his best-man, Sean, in short, clipped sentences. He'd think that she'd run away, decided not to go through with it.

And of course she couldn't do that. Not now, not after all this money and expense and the trouble so many people had gone to. It would break his heart too. He loved her. She knew he did.

Straightening her spine and tilting her chin just like her mother, Megan stepped forward.

Georgie bustled behind her, scooping up pink and white bouquets, a purse of essentials and Gucci's diamanté lead that Brendon had forgotten.

Megan went carefully down the grand staircase, holding onto the mahogany banister with one hand and raising the front of her dress with the other. It was precarious not being able to see the steps or her feet, and she had a weird sensation of not knowing where she was.

"Ah, my darling."

She smiled at her father and sister who were waiting at the bottom of the stairs. Her father had fastened his jacket around his rotund belly and his buttonhole was a little askew—no doubt he'd been fiddling with it since her mother had left only seconds ago.

Olivia did indeed look stunning. All grown up and with a healthy Australian glow. Her dress fitted her to perfection and her hair tumbled over her slender shoulders.

"What do you think?" Megan asked, sweeping her hand down her own dress.

"Absolutely beautiful," her dad replied.

"Like a princess," Olivia said.

"That's what I said." Brendon appeared at her side and cupped her elbow, supporting her. "A fairy princess."

"Is that Grammy's tiara?" Olivia asked.

Megan nodded.

"I love it. Can I wear it one day?"

"Of course." Megan hoped her father wouldn't cry at the sight of his mother's wedding day piece. She was wearing it in the picture that had always taken pride of place in the hallway cabinet.

"Well, I'm sure she'd be very happy to see you with it on today," he said then pressed his lips together and nodded vigorously.

"Come on, Dad, let's not get sentimental," Megan said, setting a quick kiss to his warm cheek. "We're late, no time for that."

"Yes, yes, of course," he said firmly.

"I'll see you there." Olivia took her bouquet from Georgie. "Mum is waiting outside for me. I said I'd go with her."

"Yes of course." Megan gave her a quick hug. "I'm so glad you're here and you look so pretty."

"Thank you, and me too." She smiled. "I wouldn't have missed my big sister getting married for the world."

Her father held out the crook of his arm. "To the church we go, Miss Winter."

They walked into the spring sunshine and were greeted by a white Rolls Royce complete with top-hatted driver. Pink ribbons fed from the silver lady on the front to the wing mirrors and fluttered slightly in the breeze.

It took both Georgie and Brendon's help for Megan to get into the car. The dress needed to be folded together and squashed through the doorway. Fortunately it didn't seem to have any creasing tendencies, it simply sprung into a big bouffant whenever it was permitted to and used up all the available space.

Her father sat beside her, and she leaned across to straighten his rose, spreading the delicate fern fronds behind it onto the material of his jacket.

"So how is the shoe business going?" he asked as the car pulled away.

"What? You really want to talk about that now?" Megan said, then laughed, surprised at this choice of subject.

"Well yes. Your mother and I are very proud that you finally bit the bullet and branched out on your own. You've always been such a girly girl, into your shoes and handbags, we're not surprised it's the route you've taken."

"I couldn't imagine doing anything else now." Megan thought back to when she'd been a little girl, she'd never liked her feet, always longed for grown-up, tanned feet with painted nails that looked good in high heels, fancy strapped buckles and sparkly sandals. She was a shoe and bag girl for sure, but if push came to shove it was shoes, glamorous stilettos in particular that made her heart flutter and she'd been known to spend far too much money on a perfect pair that called to her from a shop window.

"You've been designing for a long time now," her father went on, "it seems right that you're independent and you keep ownership of your designs rather than working for someone else."

"It's been scary, to be honest, getting a business loan from the bank and setting up independently but it's starting to pay off. The designs are being well received, the manufacturers are taking me more seriously, finally, and I'm getting several regular orders and hoping for more." She paused. "I've got big plans you know, Dad. I won't stop at the high street. I want Harrods, Selfridges, Rodeo Drive. I'm going to have my shoes featured at London Fashion week. They'll be fighting for them on the catwalks in Milan and selling out on 5th Avenue." She smiled but there was determination behind her words. Megan had big dreams for her designs, she wanted Winter Shoes to be a household name—in every household. She wanted Oscar winners, Hollywood stars, supermodels to all be clamouring to wear her shoes."

"I don't doubt for a second that you'll make it my darling, the world had better watch out." He squeezed her arm. "And advertising?" he asked, ever the businessman. "How is that coming on?"

"Brendon is helping me out with that. It's his speciality and a big push is next on my to-do list. After I get back from honeymoon, that is. Before the end of the year everyone who is anyone will own a pair of Winter Shoes. They'll be the talk of the town."

"Yes, you'll be juggling married life and your career then."

"Do you think it will be a juggle?"

"Knowing Dylan, he'll demand a good proportion of your time. Dinner on the table, shirts ironed, boots polished."

Boots polished?

Oh God, was that really what she'd be doing? She didn't want to polish clunky, big boots! She loved spending her time designing and manufacturing beautiful, delicate stilettos and sandals—shoes that were not simply something to wear but something to treasure. Her shoes made heads turn, they made memories, they made everyone wish they owned a pair.

"Ah, here we are," her father said.

"Already?"

The car drew to a halt outside the small Norman church and the driver killed the engine. The sound of the ringing bells filled her ears, their clanging a series of long, low notes that merged into a heavy drone.

Megan stared out of the window at the graveyard. The grass, dotted with daisies, was lush green thanks to a few days of rain last week. A wonky gravestone with a bunch of dead carnations at its base caught her attention.

Beryl Simmons. 1939-2009. Devoted wife of Bernard Simmons.

Devoted wife. Was that all Beryl had been? Did the words *devotion* and *wife* define Mrs Simmons? It seemed they did, in death at least. But what else had she done with her life? Had she achieved her potential?

"Time to do this," her father said, holding out his hand.

Megan stepped out and her heels sank in the gravel. She worried for the delicate soles that had a layer of gold glitter on them—her unique selling point. The gravel wouldn't do it any good at all, and would likely scratch the heels.

"Turn around," Brendon called, rushing from the car that had just pulled in behind the Rolls Royce. "You need fluffing, you're all flat. Flat as a bloody ironing board."

Megan did as instructed while Brendon one-handedly—because Gucci was still tucked under his other arm—plumped up the dress to even more enormous proportions.

"Here," Georgie said, thrusting the bigger of the two bouquets at Megan. "Don't forget this."

"Thanks." Megan wished she had a drink of water, her mouth was dry. The sun was beating down on her. She lifted the flowers to her nose and breathed deeply. They smelt fresh and powdery and the petals were so fragile. "Where's Olivia?"

"Waiting for us at the door," Brendon said, hopping around her, checking the dress. "You're good to go. Go make that man happy."

"Yes. Okay." She nodded seriously.

"And enjoy it," Georgie said. "Smile. It's not supposed to be an ordeal. You're marrying the man you love. The man you want to spend the rest of your life with."

"I know. Yes...you're right." That was how she had to look at it—she was marrying the man she loved. Why was she nervous? Why were those damn butterflies stalking her? It was only Dylan in there waiting for her. It wasn't as if he were a monster or a beast. This was real life, not a fairy tale where she was being forced to marry an ogre, or a horror story and she was wedding a madman. It was just Dylan.

She smiled at her dad and hooked her hand through the crook of his offered arm.

Georgie, Brendon and Gucci raced off ahead.

Megan and her father followed. Each step put her teeth on edge because all she could think of was the sparkle coming off her heels and being left on the gravel. No use to anyone, and the prettiness of the soles gone.

The bells stopped as they reached the entrance and the first chords of the Wedding March struck up. Before her was the aisle lined with pink bows. The pews were full to the brim and many of the congregation wore hats, making it seem even more crowded. The vicar stood at the end and nodded in greeting then spoke to someone to his left—Dylan, Megan presumed—with a reassuring smile.

Brendon, Olivia and Georgie walked down the aisle, slowly, Brendon scattering pink rose petals as he went. He flicked his wrist in an over-exaggerated way and the petals flew high before settling on the red carpet. Some landed on Gucci, who trotted alongside him on his posh lead with his tail in the air—he didn't seem to mind.

"Good luck."

Megan looked at her dad. "Thanks."

Did she need luck for the next half an hour or for the rest of her life?

He pressed a kiss to her cheek and they stepped forward. As the familiar music filled her ears, she pulled in a deep breath. Her shoes were high and she felt a little unsteady. But it was okay, she had her dad to hold onto.

The crowd turned to look at her. She smiled at Aunt Sharon and Uncle Paul then saw some girls from her old office—all wearing fabulous designer dresses from this season's line. She smiled shyly as she walked past. Her twin cousins turned, both looking handsome in suits and with their gelled hair shaped identically in right-sided partings. They had partners with them, and one was holding a child.

On and on she went. The aisle had felt small when they'd been to church in the past but now it seemed to be extending forever. The muscles in her belly quivered—she should have eaten rather than just drunk two glasses of champagne during the course of the morning.

Megan squeezed her father's arm and smiled at her mother who was dabbing her cheek with a pink handkerchief.

With each step, the dress billowed out around her feet. She watched it for a moment, studying how the petals Brendon had scattered shifted in the breeze it made, then she looked up.

Dylan stood next to the vicar. His feet were hip-width apart and his arms rod-straight, fists clenched. He'd had his hair cut, shorter than normal, and a sheen of sweat sat on his brow, highlighted by the sunlight pouring in from a stained-glass window to his right.

He shifted from one foot to the other and a tight smile spread on his face. He gave a small, approving nod.

Megan slowed a little, her heart rate quickening.

This was it. He was here, she was here.

It was time to get married.

She glanced at Sean who stood at Dylan's side. He was fiddling with his tie and was paler than usual.

God, he's as nervous as me.

But what did Sean have to be nervous about? It wasn't him getting hitched. Promising to love and honour another human being for the rest of his life.

She turned her attention back to Dylan and came to a halt in front of him.

"Take care of my girl," her dad said quietly then released Megan's arm. "We love you," he said, smiling at her and stepping away.

Megan had a sudden urge to grab him back to her, make him stay close and stroke her hair the way he used to when she was a little girl and feeling afraid of the dark, or going to a new school.

But of course she didn't. Instead, she swallowed down a bite of bile and passed her bouquet to Georgie as planned. She then turned to the vicar.

"Hello, Megan," he said warmly.

"Hi." She liked him. He was a kind, softly spoken man who gave off an air of concern and tenderness.

"Are you okay?"

"Yes, fine, thank you."

He studied her for a moment, his expression serious, then nodded and looked down at the book he held open.

Megan had a sudden feeling of emptiness—without the flowers to hold she didn't know what to do with her hands.

She looked up at Dylan.

He was smiling at her.

A sense of relief went through her. He liked how she looked—the dress, the hair, the makeup—good, she'd pleased him. Dylan wasn't fun to be around when he was in a bad mood and she really wanted him to be in a good mood, on this, their special day.

"We are gathered here today..." the vicar started.

Megan squeezed her nails into her palms.

Is this how she'd feel for the rest of her life? Wondering if Dylan was happy with her? If she'd done the right thing, worn the right clothes, spoken the correct words?

Her stomach churned over again. She could feel sweat prickling under her arms and in her cleavage. The dress felt too big and hot, stifling even.

The corset was making it hard to breathe.

The vicar was talking about the sanctity of marriage, the joining of a man and woman before God.

Dylan was staring at her and biting on his bottom lip. His eyes were narrowed as if trying to see into her mind.

And what was it he'd see?

Terror.

The acknowledgement of that emotion was like a real physical punch to the guts. Megan wavered, her balance going off kilter for a split second.

Dylan reached out and gripped her arm, tight.

"Megan, what's the matter?"

"I…?"

The vicar paused.

"What is it?" Dylan asked, frowning.

Megan couldn't say anything. She looked up at his face—there was concern there yes, but also irritation. She wasn't behaving as she should.

"I'm a little…hot…" she whispered.

"Everyone is. It's a hot day."

So she just had to cope, did she? Despite the fact she was wearing a dress that weighed a ton and a corset that meant her lungs were only functioning at half-normal capacity.

Cope.

Yes, that's what Dylan always expected her to do. Like last month when she'd ordered a meal that hadn't quite been cooked. He hadn't wanted to make a fuss because it was a friend's restaurant, so she'd had to eat around the pink bit in the chicken breast. When they'd gone on holiday and their seats had been separated. She'd had to sit long haul next to a stinky fat man who hadn't stopped talking while Dylan had sat and watched a movie with extra leg room by the emergency escape—but it didn't bother him that they'd had to sit apart. He hadn't even mentioned it.

And what about the time his mother had bought her perfume that had brought her out in a rash, yet he still insisted she wear it when they went to dinner, so that she didn't appear ungrateful—she wasn't ungrateful, she just didn't think hives were particularly attractive.

"And so now, we come to the point in the service," the vicar said in a loud voice, "that I must ask anyone who has any reason that this couple may not be wed in holy matrimony to speak up now of forever hold their peace..."

Silence fell over the church.

A long, oppressive absence of noise.

"I do!"

Megan gasped and clamped her hand over her mouth.

"What?" Dylan said, his eyes widening.

"I do," Megan said again, removing her hand and tipping her chin up. It had been her who had spoken and she could hardly believe it. It hadn't even been a conscious decision, it just *was*, it had just happened. She couldn't marry the man standing before because she didn't love him enough.

And he didn't love her enough.

Or if he did, he didn't know how to show it.

"What are you saying?" he asked, shaking his head, his cheeks flushing.

"I can't marry you, Dylan. I'm sorry."

He wiped his brow. "You're just hot, confused. How much champagne have you had?" He threw a scathing look in Brendon's direction.

"I am hot and I have had a glass or two of champagne, but that doesn't change the fact I can't marry you, Dylan. I'm really, really sorry."

Her eyes stung, her chest ached from pushing up against the corset but the weight that had settled in her belly was lifting. It was like she was getting lighter, floating. She'd released the truth that had been sneaking around her psyche for too long and it was a wonderful, freeing feeling.

"So, er...what..." asked the vicar, "do you want to do?" He looked at Dylan.

"Well clearly she's not thinking straight," Dylan said, wafting his hand at Megan as if dismissing what she'd said.

"I am. I'm thinking perfectly straight. For the first time in a long time, in fact."

Dylan's mouth twisted, as though he was in pain.

Megan hated that she'd done this to him, created this moment for him to live through. But she had to be true to herself. Her parents had just told her they were proud of her, of the woman she'd become.

And that woman didn't need Dylan.

She didn't need to be told what to do, or spend her time worrying about a grown man's mood swings.

She glanced at her mother. Her cheeks were red and her eyes wide.

She set her attention on her father—his expression was serious but, as ever, his eyes held love.

Brendon had his teeth gritted and one hand clasped beneath his chin and Georgie had pressed her palm to her chest, over her heart.

Megan knew what she was doing would alienate one side of the church. She would become a hated woman, the evil witch who broke Dylan's heart. But that couldn't be helped.

It was the way it had to be.

"Megan, come on, let's get this done then we can get out of here and talk."

"Talk?" she asked.

"Yes, talk."

"Talk as in you tell me what a silly little girl I've been. That I should just get on with it and take what life gives me—"

"Megan." Dylan's voice was stern. "What's brought this on?"

"I can't... I can't do it..." As she spoke, a sob erupted. She wrenched her arm from Dylan's grip and turned towards the church door. Hastily she scooped up her dress, gripping the delicate material and hoisting it to her knees.

She had to get out of there. It was suffocating—she couldn't be herself while she stood next to Dylan in that church.

She'd die if she had to for another second.

A rapid injection of energy, adrenaline, spurted into her system and she raced forward as fast as she could on her heels.

Olivia's shocked face whizzed by her peripheral vision, as did Dylan's mother's.

Suddenly she stumbled. Her ankle turned and a streak of pain dashed through her tendons as her heel tipped. Her shoe fell off and her bare foot landed on the petal-strewn aisle. But she didn't let the loss of a shoe stop her, it could have been so much more that she'd lost—herself.

So she continued to run, lopsidedly, but still, she didn't slow down. The brightness outside was what she needed, the caress of the sun, the birdsong. The heavy stone walls of the church and the golden ring that Sean had in his top pocket were like prison bars, handcuffs.

And she wouldn't be held captive.

Not by anyone.

3

"Well sit me sideways on a bike," Brendon said. "I never knew you had so much crap, Megan Rose Winter. You're a secret hoarder." He shook his head and tutted. "You'll end up being on one of those shows where you're living in a tiny burrow in a mouldy kitchen surrounded by junk you just can't bear to throw away."

Megan shrugged and looked around at the bags and boxes in her open-plan apartment. "It might be crap, but it's *my* crap." She grinned. It was mainly shoes, paperwork and a mountain of clothes. Brendon was just grumpy because he'd had to help carry it in from Georgie's car and he'd got sweaty. His brow and nose were also shiny. "And this is only what I had at Dylan's, this place is still full of my stuff, you know. I didn't take everything there. What do you think is in those cupboards?"

"Tasteful attire like this." He lifted a leopard skin sandal into the air—the underside was golden and glittery, except where it had worn on the ball of the sole.

"Hey, every woman should have leopard skin print sandals," Megan said, snatching it off him and dropping it back into the box. She was damn proud of that sandal and it was selling well.

"It's bloody freezing in here," Georgie said, double wrapping a scarf around her neck. "It's supposed to be August."

"I'll put the heating on." Megan went to the thermostat and fiddled with it. "It has been empty for months, and this room doesn't get much sun." She glanced out of her ground-floor window at the small strip of grass then the road. "And it will soon be September."

"Was it April you moved in with Dylan?" Georgie asked.

"Yes, that's right. He proposed on the first."

"April Fool's Day," Brendon said then laughed. "But who was the fool."

"I guess we both were."

Georgie looked sympathetic. "Five months was obviously enough to put you off Dylan for life, though, Megan."

Megan pulled a face. Ten days on from jilting her fiancé in front of all their family and friends and the guilt hadn't lessened. But the lighter feeling hadn't faded either—she still felt floaty, free, as if she could fly. She could do anything, order what she had an appetite for in a restaurant, go and see whichever movie took her fancy and throw all the hours she wanted into Winter Shoes. If she did a twelve or thirteen-hour day that was fine, she didn't have to make allowances for Dylan's moodiness if she was late or didn't have the energy to be bubbling with enthusiasm about his day.

Yes. She knew she'd made the right decision. Hard as it had been, she was one hundred per cent thankful that she wasn't Mrs Dunkin-Buckshaw and fresh from sunning herself in Mexico right now.

Her would-be husband would likely have been moaning the whole time about the foreign food, the size of the hotel room, the weather and calling home every day to keep his mother happy.

Sure, her flat might be a bit cold, she had a ton of stuff to sort through and the place needed a really good clean but it was hers and, what's more, she was still her own woman. Thank goodness she hadn't sold it.

It had been a damn close call.

Too close for comfort, in fact.

"I bumped into Sean yesterday," Georgie said, "at Tesco. He'd just got back from Mexico. I asked him how Dylan had been while they were there."

"Do you know what...?" Brendon asked, pulling a bottle of sauvignon blanc from a paisley rucksack. He dug deeper and pulled out a twisty brown dog chew. "Here, Gucci, here you go, poppet."

Gucci jumped from the sofa and ran over, tongue hanging out and feet going so fast he nearly fell over them.

"What?" Megan fiddled with the silver heart pendant she liked to wear—a present from her parents when they'd emigrated. "Do we know what?"

"I'd go for a bit of Sean, he's hot." Brendon licked his lips and nodded. "Mmm, yeah I would. Last time I saw him he was wearing this little vesty top and shorts that showed off thick thighs, hairy too, you know."

"Really?" Georgie said. "Isn't he a bit brawn and muscle for you? I thought you liked the more cultured look?"

Brendon shrugged and reached for three glasses from the kitchen cupboard. "Maybe I'd like to get me a bit of rough."

"You would not." Megan looked at his slight frame. Brendon wasn't skinny but he didn't exactly ooze muscle definition either, and his pale skin, sprinkle of freckles and hair that could only be described as ginger gave him a delicate appearance.

"Hey, don't be judgy." Brendon unscrewed the lid of the wine and set it on the counter. "I might enjoy some hanky-panky, hanky-spanky." He made a show of whacking his palm on his buttocks and jiggling his hips. "Oh yes, oh yes, oh yes, ohhhh..."

"Shut up," Georgie said, laughing. "Sean goes to the gym most nights for about three hours, he'd snap you in half with one hefty spank."

"And break your bones," Megan added.

"I'm tougher than I look." Brendon pouted then shoved up the sleeve on his T-shirt and flexed his biceps. "See. Bulging."

"We're very impressed," Megan said, nodding intently. "Now pour the wine, then we'll be even more impressed."

"Yes, ma'am. Bossy these days, aren't you?"

Megan looked at Georgie and pulled down the corners of her mouth. "I kind of want to know what Sean said about Dylan, but also I don't. I've been thinking about him since I knew they got back."

"Well don't find out then," Georgie said, taking a glass of wine from Brendon and shrugging. "Simple."

"How about you tell me, Georgie," Brendon said. "Then I can decide if Megan needs to know. I'll sift the information for her."

"You'll tell her everything anyway, whether she needs to know or not," Georgie said. "You won't be able to help yourself."

"True." Brendon nodded and passed Megan a glass of wine. "I wouldn't." He took a drink for himself. "So here's to finding out how truly broken his heart is."

"It's not funny," Megan said. "I feel really bad about it all. No one should have to go through what I did to him."

"I know you feel bad, Megan, but it's happened and the fact is, he didn't deserve you and now he needs to man-up and move on."

"He *thought* he deserved me." Megan took a sip of wine then looked between her two best friends as they glanced at each other, their lips pressed tight.

"What?" Megan asked. "What aren't you saying?"

"Nothing," Georgie said, before gulping back a mouthful of sauvignon. "Oh, that's nice. From New Zealand, is it?"

"Yes, not sure what region. Shall I look?" Brendon went to reach for the bottle.

"No, stop stalling." Megan frowned. "What aren't you saying?" Megan paused. "Brendon?"

"Well…" He drew the word out and rolled his eyes.

"What? Tell me."

"We never liked him," Georgie said. "Shit!" She pressed her lips tight together and closed her eyes.

"Oh, Georgie Porgy Pudding and Pie," Brendon exclaimed, suppressing a grin. "Really, how could you? What a thing to say."

"You never liked Dylan?" Megan asked slowly. "Is that the truth?"

Georgie took several more big gulps of wine then held her glass towards Brendon.

He topped it up.

"I'm sorry, Megan," she said. "I shouldn't have mentioned that."

"It's okay." Megan rubbed her hand over her forehead. "But…I mean…what didn't you like about him?"

"It was the way he spoke to you, mainly," Brendon said. "And how he told you to behave, ordered for you when we went out to eat, insisted on you wearing certain things that, quite frankly, darling, weren't particularly flattering."

Megan opened her mouth then shut it again.

Really?

Brendon had seen all that?

"He just didn't seem to love you for you," Georgie said, her voice gentle. She set down her wine and took Megan's hand. "And we do love you. We love how you laugh and speak and dress. How you get completely over-excited about Christmas and birthdays, how you always drop money into the hat belonging to that busker by the station even though he's always singing off key. The fact you're shoe crazy and cry sometimes when it hurts so much that your family live on the other side of the world."

"And even when your roots need doing, and you're cranky because it's the time of the month, we love you," Brendon said. "When you tell your awful jokes we don't laugh at them, we laugh *with you*."

Megan juddered out a breath.

Her friends had just listed all the things about her that had irritated Dylan. There were many more—it seemed she had really got on his nerves.

So why had he wanted to marry her so badly?

"The thing is it was him who needed to change," Georgie said, rubbing her thumb over Megan's knuckles. "People who truly love you have no desire to change you. They love you for all of your imperfections, that's the definition of love. Taking the good with the bad, taking everything that person has to offer."

"Is that how you love Tom?" Megan asked.

"Yes, absolutely." Georgie smiled, the way she always did when his name was mentioned. "To be honest, his feet smell after he's been on the construction site all day, but that's okay, at least he's done an honest day's work. And his obsession with war films is driving me insane, but that's fine, because he has issues with my *Downton* obsession, so it's live and let live." She shrugged. "Love is about compromise too. It can't just be how one person in the relationship wants it. It's how you both want it—that's how you become an equal couple."

"And I know Dylan and you had great chemistry in the bedroom," Brendon said. "But you know, will he still be getting it up in forty years' time?" He helped himself to more wine. "Chances are he'll be watching *Question Time* and plucking hairs from his ears and sniffing his own farts."

"Ick," Megan said, screwing up her nose.

"See, my point exactly. If the thought of your beloved plucking hairs from their ears and farting doesn't turn you on, then it's a no brainer."

"Well—" Georgie started.

"It's happened now," Megan said firmly, "and there's no going back, but—"

"But what?" Georgie asked.

"If either of you ever think these things again, or anything similar about the next guy I meet, because I seriously hope I won't be a spinster forever—"

"Oh, what a ridiculous thing to say." Brendon tutted dramatically.

"Well, you never know." Megan sighed.

"We promise to tell you, cross our hearts," Georgie said. "We should have, and I'm sorry." She looked at Brendon.

"Yeah, we should have," Brendon said, shaking his head. "But you seemed so in love with him. So *consumed* by him."

"I thought I was. Dylan is a force to be reckoned with. He is a whirlwind of determined energy. He knows how he wants things to be and he makes it happen. I got swept up in that, in pleasing him, in trying to achieve his idea of perfection."

"Well it seems he's not best pleased now, and everything is far from perfect in Dylanland."

"Oh, dear." Megan's heart sank. She'd had one painful, apologetic conversation on the phone the day after the non-wedding. He'd begged, cried, been angry and had finally sworn that he'd make her see sense. In the end she'd put the phone down and had had no contact since. She'd taken her stuff from his house when she'd known he was away then had posted the key through the letterbox. "You best tell me."

"Oh yes, spill the beans," Brendon said. "God, I can't believe he went on the honeymoon."

"I told him to," Megan said. "Seemed silly to waste more money, and let's face it, everyone here was talking about him, he didn't need to hear it all and be pitied. Getting away seemed the best thing. I can handle the heat, it's my heat. Besides, him and Sean have always been good mates."

Georgie sighed and sat on a stool. "Yeah, well, Sean said he's in bits, but we guessed that, and it's early days."

"Yes," Brendon acknowledged. "It is very soon. He needs to grieve for our Megan."

"I'm not dead."

"You are to him."

Megan picked up her wine and took a gulp. "What else did Sean say?"

"He got a tattoo while they were on your honeymoon." Georgie tapped her chest. "Apparently it's of a rose and it's on his chest, over his heart."

"What?" Megan stood from the box she'd been perched on. "What a knob. That can't be true."

"It is. And he told Sean it was because you'd always be in his heart. Sean said he tried to stop him but there was no way on this Earth he could talk him out of it."

"That's crazy."

Brendon spun his index finger by his ear and made a bird-whistle sound. "Cuckoo."

"He wouldn't have done that if we'd got married. He always said he didn't like tattoos."

"But you didn't get married and it seems being rejected has sent him into a tailspin," Georgie said.

"I didn't reject him, I just…didn't want to marry him."

"Same thing." Brendon sat on the sofa. Gucci jumped onto his lap and started licking his chin.

"He got wrecked, every night, Sean said. Spent the whole time hatching plans to get you back. Trying to figure out what he'd done wrong, what he needed to change."

"Shit!" Megan placed her palm over her forehead. Sure, he'd been upset when she'd spoken to him on the phone, but he hadn't sounded like he was that mental.

"Sean said it was the, and I quote, 'worst fucking holiday of his life'."

"I bet it was," Brendon said. "A week with miserable Dylan. I'd have hung myself from the balcony even if there was all the free tequila I could drink."

"God, I felt bad before, now I feel terrible." Megan shook her head.

"No, you mustn't," Georgie said. "And I didn't tell you so you'd feel bad, only so that, you know, if he calls or comes round, maybe drop one of us a text or something and we'll pop over. I think safety in numbers would be the best policy here."

"He'd never hurt me." Megan was shocked that they might think that.

"We know he wouldn't," Brendon said. "But still, we'd rather one of us was around if he decides he wants to…talk."

Megan glanced out of the window at the sky. It was dotted with fluffy, marshmallow clouds. Dylan might have had some odd quirks and been controlling, but he'd never made her worry about her personal safety. "Okay. I'll drop a text, but I doubt he'll show up. He knows it's over."

"We just don't want him round here plastered, thinking he can persuade you to go back to him," Brendon said.

"And he is very persuasive," Georgie added.

"I know, but it's fine. He'll meet someone else and it will all work itself out. I'll be a distant memory." Damn, she hoped that was the truth. Really and truly she did.

"Talking of meeting someone else," Brendon said, puffing up his chest and sitting straighter. "Now you're a single gal, have you seen Hot Guy lately?" He waggled his eyebrows.

Hot Guy. Oh yeah, now he *was* hot. Scorching, in fact. Megan had seen him regularly over the last few months wandering past her office morning and evening, and occasionally dropping into Frank's Bar for a drink. She'd never spoken to him, though, just enjoyed his tall, dark handsomeness from afar. He always looked like he was deep in thought, brooding, concentrating on something important. She often wondered what was going through his mind.

Several times she'd sat in Frank's with a glass of wine and hoped he might come over and speak to her. Their eyes *had* met—it wouldn't have been a ridiculous thing to happen. But he never had, he'd always stayed seated and apparently listening to the live music or mulling over his day. If she'd had her engagement ring on she would have understood the lack of contact.

"Yes, I did see him actually," she said. "He came past at his usual time on Friday and ducked into Frank's."

"Mmm, and was he looking all dashing and pant-droppingly sexy?" Brendon licked his lips salaciously.

Megan's heart sank at the memory. "No, well yes, but—"

"There's a but?" Brendon slapped his palm over his chest. "Oh no. Pray tell."

"Yes, last time I saw him he was with someone, a woman." Megan frowned and shook her head. "No, a girl really, well definitely legal age, you know, but she looked much too young for him. Skinny and blonde, tatty jeans and a Burberry mac."

"Ah, you see," Brendon said, shaking his head, "snooze you lose."

"Well hold your horses..." Georgie held up her hand. "There might be an explanation. Daughter, perhaps?"

"He's not *that* old," Megan said. "Anyway..." She gave a defeated sigh. "Like Brendon said, snooze you lose, and while he's been having a great time with his young hottie, I've been untangling myself from Dylan, so it obviously wasn't meant to be."

"Oh never ever say never, darling." Brendon drew a large arc in the air with his hand. "Who knows what fate has in store for you."

"It might have nothing in store for me." Megan had a sudden pang in her chest. What if she'd totally screwed up? What if Dylan was the best she was ever going to get and she'd thrown it all away? Perhaps the single life wasn't for her after all. Maybe she'd be better off married and getting on with it...

"Buck up, will you," Georgie said with an uncharacteristic forceful tone. "The world is your oyster, Megan. It's all there waiting for you, go grab it by the horns. There is absolutely nothing to stop you achieving your dreams and we know you have big dreams. Plans to take the fashion industry by storm with your fabulous shoes and knock all those other designers off their pedestals."

"Oh yeah, and we just know you can do it, wearing the best footwear out there in the process," Brendon said, holding up his wine. "So, let's drink to grabbing horns, one of my favourite pastimes. And don't think you're alone, sweetpea. Pudding and Pie here might be loved up, but me and you are gonna have so much fun and grab so many horns!"

"Hey, I can still do fun."

"Of course you can." Megan gave Georgie a quick hug. Her best friend wasn't the sort to ditch and run because she had a man in her life. They'd still spend plenty of time together, the way they always had, sharing gossip, talking through worries and having a laugh.

Megan smiled and looked between Brendon and Georgie. Her friends were right. She had to get back in the saddle. This was what running from the altar had been about, finding herself again, *being* herself again.

And damn, she was ready to take the challenge, and like Brendon had said, she'd be wearing the most fabulous shoes in the process, *her* fabulous shoes which at the moment would be the focus of her days and likely nights too.

4

Megan loved her Change Street office—it was small, cute and despite being in the City had the perfect relaxed vibe for letting her imagination run riot. But as she let herself through the front door the next day, she felt weary and her limbs were heavy.

She'd had a restless night's sleep. Dreams of the non-wedding had swirled around her mind in disjointed tangles. One minute she'd been getting ready, Brendon fluffing up her dress and Georgie slipping on the garter, Olivia smiling at her as she walked down the stairs at the hotel. Then she'd been outside the church, her precious heels sinking in the gravel, the gravestones all around her looming large and ominous, much bigger than they really were, more like cliffs trapping her in. Suddenly she'd been at the end of the aisle, her father slipping backwards, getting smaller, her mother and Olivia shrinking too so that she'd been all alone with Dylan. The emotions of the moment had raced through the dream, tightening her throat, squeezing her chest. The vicar's voice had boomed. Dylan had gripped her arms. In a flash she'd been running, racing, charging down the aisle towards the outside, to the fresh air so she could breathe. But as she'd held her dress high, gripping the taffeta, she'd stumbled, one heel caught in the ground, fastening, sticking to something she couldn't see in her dream. It had held her there, solid. She'd yanked and pulled, had put all her effort into releasing her foot but it had been no good. She'd been trapped. Trapped forever in the church with everyone looking at her and Dylan walking to get her, pick her up and make her his.

She'd woken hot, sweaty and breathless with her pulse loud in her ears. It had taken a few moments to realise it had all been a dream and not true. She hadn't fallen in the aisle, sure she had stumbled and lost a shoe, but she'd made it out into the open. She'd found freedom and claimed it. The bruise on her twisted ankle had lasted for several days, but at least some weird Devil hands hadn't reached from the red carpet on the church aisle and held her fast.

Thank goodness.

A pile of mail sat on her mat. Hopefully she'd have some orders, the more the better. Now was the time—as Georgie and Brendon had said—to throw herself into work, and luckily there was plenty to be getting on with.

She reached for her mail and, as she straightened, a shoe fell from her bag. It was her bridal shoe, the one remaining stiletto. She'd picked it up on a whim when she'd left home that morning, wondering in some crazy moment if having it in the house had been the reason she'd had the dream. She couldn't quite bring herself to throw it away—she was really pleased with its design—but she didn't want to live with it either. Georgie would say her thoughts were irrational and that inanimate objects didn't hold bad luck or bad spirits. But Megan couldn't help feeling a little superstitious about the shoe that had made her feel like Cinderella—except the prince she'd ran from was no charmer and she definitely didn't want him to come looking for her.

"Morning, Megan, how are you?"

She retrieved the shoe and turned to the doorway. "Hi, Ted, good thanks."

Ted smiled and fiddled with his tie. He worked at Crawford Estate Agents which leased the office next to hers and he always smelt of strong aftershave that lingered in the air after he'd left.

"Didn't get much of a tan, did you?" He laughed. "Spend the whole week in the hotel room?" He winked and gave a knowing nod. "Can't be bad."

Shit.

"I, er…" She paused. "I didn't go on honeymoon."

"Oh?" He looked confused and his smile fell. "You didn't?"

"Nope." She held up her left hand, showing off her bare ring finger. "Didn't get married at all in fact, so there was no point in having a honeymoon."

"Well I'll be buggered." He shook his head and frowned. "And here was me thinking you were a new bride."

"Not a bride, just same old me, well, minus the fiancé."

"But… Why…?" He hesitated. "No, I'm sorry. I shouldn't ask. That was rude of me."

"It's fine." She might as well say—she spoke to the guys in the estate agents most days as she was coming and going and it would be no secret that she was a jilter. "I guess I got cold feet." She held up the shoe and huffed. "Very cold. Stone cold."

"Blimey."

"I just couldn't… I suppose I wasn't ready to settle down."

"Well, your poor jilted groom's loss is every other man's gain."

"That's kind of you to say." Megan smiled. "I really should get on."

"Yes, yes of course, but you know. If you need anything, even if you just want to join me and the boys for a coffee break, come round, you know you're always welcome, we love catching up with what's hot in the shoe world."

"That's kind." Megan rested her hand on his arm. "I might just do that."

She turned, went into Winter Shoes headquarters then shut the door behind her. Ted was kind and well meaning. He was older than her and married with two kids, but always took the time to say hello. In fact, all the guys in the estate agents were nice. They all spoke to her, often asked if she wanted lunch picking up if they were going on a run to Subway and had even invited her on their staff night out at Christmas—not that she'd gone. Dylan had sulked all evening when she'd said she was thinking about it. Now that she thought about it, Dylan had sulked whenever she'd mentioned the Crawford Estate Agents. He'd had an issue with the fact that she worked in close proximity with a bunch of nice looking, nice smelling blokes.

As if she'd have dated any of them! She'd been with Dylan. Megan wasn't in the habit of two-timing. Finish one relationship before starting another had been very wise advice from her mother many years ago and had stood her in good stead. Dylan's unjustified jealous sulks had been wearisome to say the least. At the time he'd said it was just because he cared about her, now she thought it showed nothing more than childish insecurity on his behalf.

She flicked on the kettle then placed the single bridal shoe on a high shelf, beside the window. She'd come back to it, in a few weeks, work on designing more bridal shoes from that one idea but change it slightly. She wouldn't like to jinx anyone else's wedding by having an exact replica.

After booting up her computer, she made a green tea then sat at her desk. Over the next three hours she tackled her inbox and juggled what was urgent and what could wait. Her new ankle boots weren't selling as well as she'd hoped and a box of prototypes couldn't be located—seemingly lost in transit. It was all hassle, things that an assistant could do in reality.

Georgie worked in human resources, for an agency, and had been pestering Megan to take on a secretary. Megan wondered if the time had finally arrived to bite the bullet and allow someone else to hold the reins for a while. That way she would be freed up to work on designing and getting new sales avenues set up.

Mmm. Tomorrow, yes, she'd speak to Georgie about it tomorrow, or maybe the next day. When she had a spare minute.

A message from her mother popped onto her iPhone, letting her know they were back in Sydney and loved her very much. Megan held back a tear she knew could easily spring forth. She'd spent as much time with them as possible while they'd been in London. She'd felt cocooned in their love and support this last week and was so glad of their understanding.

But now, after teary goodbyes at Heathrow, they were on the other side of the world—again.

She stood and went to the lead-paned window. Across the cobbled street, nestled between a private home and a discreet and very exclusive spa retreat, was Frank's Bar. The dark curtains were permanently shut and the paintwork on the door and window frames a glossy black. Two stone planters held twisted topiary trees either side of the entrance step.

It wasn't a very inviting bar from the outside, but Megan knew that once within its warm depths, she could relax for an hour or so. Each evening live musicians performed, nothing crazy or loud, just gentle jazz or a pianist with a few melodic songs. She knew the waiters to look at if not by name, and had a favourite seat in the far left corner, in the shadows. She'd sat there often before going home to Dylan, enjoying a glass of wine in peace before jumping on the Tube and coping with the rat race.

Maybe she'd go there tonight, have a cold sauvignon and enjoy the ambience. Perhaps Hot Guy would be there. He always made for nice scenery. No, what was the point in thinking that? As Brendon had said, snooze you lose, and as she'd been planning a wedding that was never to be, Hot Guy had nabbed himself a young hottie to hang off his arm.

She sighed and returned to her laptop. Pulling a muesli bar and a banana from her bag, she got back to work. There was so much to do. Samples to look through and decisions to make about her spring collection. Orders to chase up, manufacturers to pay, and an advertising slogan to decide upon. Brendon was helping her more and more with advertising—being in marketing, it was a definite skill he had and was unendingly generous with. But she knew she'd kept him waiting for a while now, and she needed to stop stalling and get on with publicity, keep up with production and do that 'push' he kept talking about.

The day rolled past quickly, each hour surprising her with the speed in which it slipped away. The estate agents went home—she saw Ted walk past her window with his head down against a light drizzle that filled the evening air.

"Time for me to go to," she said, shutting down her computer. She stood and looked at the bar. She should probably just go home. But why? What for? Her flat was empty, not even a cat to greet her. There was no rush, and besides, she could do exactly what she wanted now, when she wanted.

"Georgie." She remembered Georgie saying she was working nearby today, interviewing or something. Quickly she picked up her phone and sent a text.

Fancy meeting me at Frank's for a GOW?

She hit send, and as she did her mobile rang.

"Hello."

"Hello, Miss Winter."

"Yes."

"This is Ria & Hankley, I'm afraid we're going to have to reverse our decision about stocking next season's designs. We put it to the board but we simply don't have the shelf space for up-and-coming designers."

Her heart sank. "Oh, but…"

"I know, and I apologise if you'd got your hopes up but the decision is final."

"What about next season?" There had to be some hope. She couldn't just let it end like this. Didn't they know she was the next big thing of the shoe world?

"I really couldn't say. Have a nice evening."

The line went dead. Megan stared at it. *Of all the…*

"Bloody hell." She sighed. It had been a big break to get shelf space at Ria & Hankley and she'd been incredibly excited—it would have been the boost her designs needed to really get noticed. How was she ever going to achieve her goals if she couldn't get her stuff into the best windows and the most sought after shelves?

She paced the small room, dodging boxes of shoes and samples of material as she went. This really finished off the day with a bitter taste. She'd spent hours on that project and within a few seconds it was dust.

Now she definitely needed that glass of wine. She looked at her phone again. Georgie had text back.

Sure. Have to meet Tom quickly first then will see you at Frank's about 9.

Good, now at least she'd have someone to moan about Ria & Hankley to and how unfair it was that the big chains got to decide who was successful and who wasn't.

Her attention caught on a sample of cream leather that was sprinkled with sparkles. "Mmm…nice." She picked it up. It was from a new selection of testers that had arrived on her week off. She fed it through her fingers—it was soft and pliant, perfect for sandals. Quickly, she grabbed her sketchpad and pencil, sat cross-legged on the floor and began to create a perfect summer mule.

Megan drew until the light had gone and she could barely see her creation. She was squinting, trying to use the weak beam from a single streetlamp to see. She sighed and glanced at her phone.

Nine o'clock.

"Bugger." She jumped up and placed the sketchpad on her desk atop a pile of papers she'd never quite got to, several files and a bunch of magazines. First thing in the morning it would have her full attention. Absolutely.

Without bothering to flick on the desk lamp, Megan dragged a brush through her hair, applied a dash of powder and a sweep of her favourite red lipstick—thank goodness that was back in her life—then locked up.

Outside it was still and quiet. The nearby shops and the estate agents were in darkness and the drizzle fluttered past the glow of the lamp.

Megan pulled her light jacket around herself and scanned the shadows. It was so silent. Different to the day when there was always someone coming and going along the narrow street. Now it was empty—the rain and the damp had pushed everyone inside.

She took several steps forward, her heels clicking on the cobbles. A shiver went up her spine and the light rain dusted over her cheeks.

A quiet bang to her right caught her attention. She stopped and turned. A deep door recess to her left was in pitch blackness. That was where the noise had come from.

She stared at it, hoping her eyes would adjust.

Her heart raced.

Another bang and movement. An arm perhaps, moving in the shadows?

Adrenaline flooded her veins. There was someone there, she was sure of it—lurking, hiding and definitely up to no good.

Her legs were twitchy with the need for fight or flight. She tightened her grip on her purse strap over her shoulder and took several quick steps backward, closing the distance between her and Frank's Bar.

Safety.

"Who's there?" she called.

Nothing. No reply.

Had she imagined it?

She turned and hurried into the bar. The warmth and the soft lighting embraced her, as did the familiar scent of cologne and beer.

She moved through the room, glanced at the door again and narrowly missed walking into a table.

Would she be followed? Was the *thing* that was lurking going to come in here? God, she hoped not. It had seriously freaked her out.

"You all right, Miss? Look like you've seen a ghost."

"I'm fine." Megan turned her attention to the bartender who'd spoken to her. He was regular staff, she'd seen him before. "Just glad to be in here, out of the dark and the rain."

"Yeah, it's horrible out there. Usual?"

"Yes, please, make it two large."

He smiled. "Blimey, you are glad to be here."

Megan grabbed her purse and managed a tight smile. "They're not both for me. I'm meeting someone, a friend."

He nodded and reached for two glasses.

Megan checked the door again. She was being silly, wasn't she? Why would someone spend their evening hanging around a doorway in this weather? She'd worked too many hours and not had enough to eat, that was it. Her imagination, which her father had always told her was too vivid, was getting carried away and inventing stuff.

"Fifteen, please." The bartender set two glasses of wine before her. It appeared crisp and cold, the glasses misting.

Megan handed over the cash then picked up the two drinks. She headed for her favourite corner—which was thankfully free—and sat just as a pianist set up a quiet background tune.

She took a sip of her drink, rested back and let the lulling music calm her nerves. Georgie would be here soon—that was good— and at this moment in time she could do with a hug from her. Georgie gave great hugs. Plus it meant she wouldn't have to leave Frank's on her own. She'd have someone with her. She didn't fancy going out alone if her imagination was running riot.

Her phone tinkled, and as she picked it up, she cast her eye around the bar. A few regulars were there, but not Hot Guy. Not that it mattered if he was there or not, he was taken.

But he was rather lovely eye candy. Admiring from afar wasn't a sin.

"Hey, Georgie, how are you?"

"Oh my God, oh my God, oh my God, you are not going to believe this, Megan."

Georgie's excited voice was so loud Megan had to hold her phone an inch from her ear.

"What? Bloody hell, what?"

"He's just gone and done it, hasn't he?" Her voice was high-pitched, her words tumbling over into one long string of sound.

"Done what?"

"You know, and on the London Eye too, right at the top. Oh my God, oh my God."

"What, Georgie, what has *who* done on the top of the London Eye?"

"Tom, he went and did it, proposed. He tricked me onto the London Eye then when we were at the top he dropped to one knee and popped the question. He had a ring and everything, a sapphire in a platinum band, and it fits perfectly. Oh my God. Oh my God."

"Would you stop saying that... And wow, congratulations." A rush of happiness went through Megan. This was what Georgie had wanted for so long. She'd dreamt of it, hoped for it. "On the London Eye?"

"Yes, oh yes, it was so..." She sighed. "So romantic and everyone else in the pod, is that what they're called, started clapping and congratulating us, and when we got off we went for champagne and I... Oh, Megan, I'm so happy, so very happy and I love him so much. He's my everything."

"I know you do and he loves you. This is wonderful. I wish I was there to give you a hug."

"That will have to wait." She paused. "I'm sorry, I'm not going to get to Frank's."

"Of course you're not, bloody hell, you've just got engaged. What are you doing calling me, you should be jumping Tom's bones. Your new fiancé."

"Well...that is next on the agenda." She giggled. "To shag my new fiancé."

"Have you told Brendon?"

"Not yet. I wanted to tell you first."

"Ah, that's nice." Megan's heart swelled with affection. Theirs was such a special bond.

"I wanted to make sure you were okay with it, Megan?"

"Yes, of course, why wouldn't I be? I'm over the moon for you."

"Well I know you're not having a great time at the moment. And after the church and Dylan and..."

"I'm fine, in fact I couldn't be better, life is on the up, and honestly, hearing this news, well now I'm really okay, I couldn't be happier for you." Megan kept her voice light and breezy, hoping to inject enthusiasm into her words. But the truth was it did hurt, like a tiny dagger twisted in her heart. A few months ago she had been the one excited about a new ring and setting a date, and look where that had got her.

"Ah, you're the best, and it will all work out for you, I know it will."

"Absolutely it will, but before you go and…well do whatever please, please send me a picture of the ring." Megan was desperate to see it, sapphire in platinum sounded beautiful and so very perfect for Georgie. Tom did indeed know her well.

"Okay, will do."

"Now go, future Mrs Ellis, and have some fun. We'll catch up tomorrow and you can give me all the details about the proposal and I mean all, I don't want you to miss a thing out. I need to know what you were wearing, which direction he was facing when on one knee and—"

"Yes, tomorrow, all the details tomorrow." She laughed then gasped. "Tom, get off… Megan…I have to…go…"

"Okay, have fun." Megan ended the call and stared at the two huge glasses of wine.

She'd just have to drink them both.

5

Megan had just started on the second sauvignon and spent several minutes admiring the photograph Georgie had sent of her stunning ring, when she noticed the door opening and a new customer striding in.

Her senses heightened and she studied the way he walked. It was him. Hot Guy. He wore a black leather jacket, jeans and his dark hair glistened slightly as the dim overhead light caught on the tiny drips of rain.

He paused for a moment as the door shut behind him, and he scanned the bar. He seemed to exhale, as though glad to have arrived then his attention settled on her, sat in her usual spot.

For a moment, it was as if time stood still.

Their gazes connected.

Megan's heart did a little flip. There was just something about him. His handsome face always wore such a serious expression. She wondered what it took to make him smile, really smile. God, she'd love to see that.

She picked up her drink and tore her focus from him, looking instead at the pianist who was singing a slow song about a sinking boat. What was the point in wondering about his smile? He was spoken for. He smiled for someone else now.

But in her peripheral vision she could still see him—she couldn't help but surreptitiously watch him.

He walked to the bar and ordered a bottle of beer, pulling his wallet from his pocket.

There was a clatter and a bang.

Megan looked Hot Guy's way again. The barman was frantically trying to stop a bottle of beer from rolling off the wooden surface and onto the floor. A gush of froth sprayed and landed on Hot Guy's arm.

"I'm really sorry," the barman said, finally catching the stray bottle and righting it. "Really sorry, sir."

"It's okay." Hot Guy reached for some napkins and wiped his jacket. "No harm done."

"Are you sure? Is your jacket okay?" The barman appeared genuinely worried and glanced at another member of staff—his boss, perhaps.

"It's only a jacket, mate, don't worry about it." Hot Guy smiled, just a little.

Ah, so that's what he looked like when he wasn't deadly serious. His full lips stretched and small creases darted from the corners of his eyes. It wasn't a full on grin, but it was a genuine smile.

"We can get it dry-cleaned, sir."

"That really won't be necessary, I'm sure it's had beer on it in the past and lived to tell the tale."

The barman seemed to sag with relief and reached for another beer then popped the lid.

Megan thought of how Dylan had once totally over-reacted when a waiter had spilled sauce on him when they'd been out for dinner. He'd created a terrible scene in the restaurant and demanded to see the manager. He'd had his entire suit dry-cleaned at the restaurant's expense, even though it was only a very small mark on the sleeve that would have likely sponged out. Megan had sat through the whole embarrassing incident poking at her Dover sole and wishing she were invisible.

"On the house," the barman said.

"No seriously, it's all good," Hot Guy said, placing cash on the bar. He turned to Megan.

She realised that she was still staring at him. That she had been for ages. It was as if he were a magnet that drew her focus to him.

He took a sip of his beer, his attention not leaving her.

A tingle went over Megan's scalp and down her neck. There was a tightening in her belly. Damn, the guy was gorgeous and when his blue eyes settled on her, like she was the only woman in the place, it made her feel so special.

She stared down at her drink, swirling the stem between her fingers. What the hell was wrong with her? It wasn't as if she'd had to go without it for long.

"Can I join you?" A deep voice came from her left.

Before she even looked she knew it was him.

"If you want to," she said, peering up. She kept her voice deliberately cool. It was okay to admire him from afar, but he had a young girlfriend who was no doubt waiting for him in some trendy minimalist apartment and wondering what sexy lingerie to wear for him that night.

His expression faltered, but only for a second—a flash of surprise at her cool reaction maybe? He took a seat opposite her.

"Have you got company tonight or are you feeling thirsty?" He nodded at her two wine glasses.

"Both." She huffed. "I was meeting my friend and got the first round in but she's not coming now."

"Nothing wrong, I hope."

"No, on the contrary, she's just got engaged so she's busy…er…celebrating."

"How nice." He shrugged out of his jacket and rested it on the back of the chair next to him.

He wore a plain black, short-sleeved shirt with the collar undone. He had stubble on his cheeks, more than a day's growth, and it was neatly trimmed. Megan wondered if his chest had a similar sprinkle of hair, if he'd have a dark trail from navel to…

What am I doing?

The wine had gone to her head.

She pushed her drink to one side and took a deep breath. "Yes, he just proposed on the London Eye so that's all very exciting for them."

"But it means you're stood up."

"Well, I don't know about that, I just…" It was true, what could she say? She had been stood up but for the nicest possible reason.

He glanced at the pianist. "He's good. I like this one. He was playing last time I was here."

"When you were with your girlfriend, the young blonde one." Megan pressed her lips together. Damn, why did she have to sound so uptight? This was the first bloke she'd spoken to, other than her father, Brendon and the estate agents, since she'd run down the aisle. Did she have to sound so whiney?

He looked at her and tipped his head. "I'm James, by the way. James Carter."

"Nice to meet you. I'm Megan."

He took another sip of his beer. "The blonde girl. That's Roxy, my niece. She was over here from Los Angeles doing work experience with me. She headed back to the Sunshine State yesterday."

"Oh, I see." His *niece*. Well, that certainly put a different slant on things. "And what is it you do, you know, that she was getting experience with?"

"I'm a director, she wants to go into journalism and thought it would be good experience." He pushed his hand through his hair which caused it to stick up slightly. "Though really I think she just enjoyed clubbing in London with new friends, that's what they do these days, the youngsters."

"How old is she?"

"Twenty."

"And very pretty."

"I suppose she is." He paused and studied Megan. "And what do you do? I'm guessing you work nearby, if this is your local haunt."

"Yes, just over the way. I design shoes."

He nodded slowly and bit on his bottom lip.

"What?" She bristled a little. Okay she was no big shot director, but she was doing okay, thank you very much. More than okay and soon she'd be flying high, she'd make sure she was.

"That explains why you always have amazing footwear," he said.

"You noticed?" He didn't strike her as the type to notice shoes. Damn it, she hoped he wasn't gay. Brendon always knew exactly what everyone had on their feet, at all times—it was, like, inbuilt in him to spot footwear. *Bugger!* And just when she'd found out Hot Guy wasn't with the pretty young blonde after all. He probably had a pretty young blond boyfriend stashed away.

"Well, I'm not usually a connoisseur of shoes, but one day last month, I did notice that you had glittery soles."

"You did?"

"Yes. Very unusual and…cute."

"Thank you. It's a trademark of mine. I love to make women feel special and sparkly when they put on my shoes. I want them to feel like they can achieve anything, reach for the stars."

"That sounds very admirable."

"It's important to feel good." She fiddled with her silver necklace, rolling the tiny heart-shaped pendant between her fingers.

"I couldn't agree more." His gaze dropped to her throat and lingered there.

His eyelids were heavy. There was a definite glimmer of interest in the depth of his pupils and he swept his tongue over his bottom lip. So he wasn't gay after all.

What is he thinking? What does he want?

She knew what she was thinking and what she wanted. That she'd quite like to feel good with Hot Guy, or James Carter, as she now knew him to be called. Her body tingled with a sudden longing for intimacy. "One day last month…" she said, repeating his words about seeing her in glittery shoes.

"I haven't been stalking you, honest," he said, "but my work has meant that I've been based nearby for a while now. I couldn't help but notice you, a beautiful woman who always sits alone."

He thinks I'm beautiful. A rush of heat flooded her cheeks and she was glad of the shadows in her tucked away corner to hide her blush. "Well, I was just, you know… I have got friends…"

"I'm sure you have. We all have reasons for wanting to sit alone sometimes."

"Why do you sit alone?"

He was quiet for a moment and glanced at the pianist again. "I guess I just need the headspace after a day at work. Can get a bit heavy sometimes."

"Oh, why is that?"

He looked back at her. "I'm working on a documentary about poverty and how it affects children, and it can get intense, here, you know?" He pressed his palm over his shirt, flattening the material to his body.

"Wow, yes, I'm sure."

He picked up his beer and drained it. "Would you like another drink?"

"No, thank you. I've had two." She glanced at the door. "I really should get going." Why? She could stay. She didn't have to get going at all.

"How are you getting home?" James asked.

"I'll walk to the main road and get a cab. That's what I usually do when I can't face the Tube." She'd run more like—she had no intention of lingering near those shadows. The thought of being out there alone on the cobbles gave her the creeps.

"I'll come with you." He reached for his coat.

"No, you don't have to."

"I insist. The old lamp posts around here are all very quaint for the tourists to admire but they don't do anything to enhance safety for women on their own."

Megan again thought of the bang she'd heard from the dark depths of the doorway. She suppressed a shiver. She would be glad of James' company if he was willing to give it. "Well, if you insist."

"I do." He stood and pulled on his jacket. His limbs were long and lean and he had a slow, controlled way of moving.

Megan slipped her light coat on then headed to the door. She nodded at the barman and raised her hand to the pianist who smiled her way, not interrupting his playing for even a moment.

"After you, Glitter," James said, reaching the door first and pulling it open.

"Glitter?"

"Yes, that's what I called you until I found out your name's Megan."

She smiled. He had a nickname for her? That was so adorable. But she'd keep the fact that she privately called him Hot Guy under wraps—for now at least.

She glanced into the darkness. There was a slight fog building up. Was there someone there?

"So is that your office?" James asked, pointing at Winter Shoes headquarters, which only consisted of one door and one window.

"Yes, it is. Only small for now but one day it will be a global empire." She laughed. "Actually, I might just grab something. I was mid flow on a new design when I had to leave earlier. I'll take it home and carry on with it later, if I don't I just know it will play on my mind."

"Your creativity doesn't switch off then?"

"No, I dream of shoes." She chuckled then stopped, thinking of the nightmare she'd had about getting her heel stuck as she ran down the aisle. "Well, you know what I mean. I adore them, they're my bread and butter and I hope my designs will lead to big things when they get noticed properly."

"I'm sure they will, you sound very passionate about your business. Come on then, you can show me your office. The place you plan to co-ordinate this world domination of the glamorous shoe industry." James set his palm against the small of her back and urged her over the cobbles.

Megan liked the feel of his hand on her, the weight of it, the span of his fingers. Damn, he could put those hands in other places and she wouldn't complain.

She was also a little lightheaded from the wine.

She found her key and unlocked the entrance.

James flicked on a light and clicked the door shut behind them. "Nice." As he had in the bar, he removed his jacket and dropped it on the chair.

"Well, like I said, it's not very big and it's a bit…messy. But it's perfectly organised, just…spread out." She reached for the blind she'd forgotten to close earlier and dropped it down to cover the window. She didn't like to think passers-by could see in and spot her designs.

He smiled and picked up a pink and silver stiletto. He turned it over, examined the base then held it to the light. "Is this one of yours?"

"Yes, that's a prototype for my summer range."

He nodded and set it on the desk.

Megan searched around for her pencil case, likely it was on the floor. It was hard to think straight with Hot Guy in her office. She couldn't deny she'd had the odd fantasy about him over the last few months, only small ones of course, because she'd been engaged. But still…

She saw her case and straightened. A slight head rush made her dizzy. She grabbed the desk.

"Hey, you okay?" He stepped up close and rested his hand on her shoulder.

"Yes…fine." She looked up at him.

Shadows sliced across his features, making them appear more angled. His eyes were dark and his lips soft and sensual.

She wondered how he'd kiss. What would those lips feel like against hers, on her body?

He didn't move. He continued to stare at her, the burning intensity in his expression heating her up from the inside out.

Is he going to kiss me?

"James?" she whispered.

"Mmm?"

"I…"

He slid his hand from her shoulder to the back of her neck, slowly, his palm soft against her skin.

Megan's breaths were light, her heart pounding. She could smell his spiced cologne and feel his body heat pouring from him.

A coil of excitement tightened inside her. She wanted him, there was no doubt about that.

And it seemed he wanted her.

He cradled the back of her skull and lowered his head.

"I've been waiting to do this for a while," he said, then pressed his lips to hers.

Megan ran her hands up his chest and gripped his shoulders. The guy could kiss—all soft and caressing—his tongue just stroking hers. She tipped her head and deepened the entry. Wanting more, wanting all of it.

He strengthened his hold, cupping her nape now and circling her waist with his other arm. A small huff left his throat as he pulled her nearer.

She touched her body to his and closed her eyes. This was a kiss of dreams, the stuff of fantasies, and it was amazing to be squeezed up against him. Toned muscle and strength surrounded her and she was so small in his embrace.

"You feel so good," he said, breaking the kiss and trailing his lips over her cheek to her ear. "Even better than I imagined."

"You imagined this?"

"Hell yeah." He scooped her up and sat her on the desk that was right behind her. A file toppled to the floor, as did a stack of papers. He moved to stand between her legs.

Oh God, is this really happening?

"I'm sure I'm not the first man to fantasise about a beautiful woman who always sits alone." He ran his fingers into the hair at her temples and forced her to tip her head and look up at him.

"What did you fantasise about doing?" Megan was floating, consumed by him. He'd fantasised about her. *Wow.*

"Can I show you?" he asked. "Rather than tell you?"

"Yes."

He kissed her again. There was less control this time. He plunged his tongue into her mouth, his breaths hard on her cheek. He eased her backwards onto the table and rested over her. A box of samples went flying and so did her stapler.

Megan couldn't care less. She was hot for him. She wrapped her legs around the back of his and pulled his shirt from his waistband. She needed flesh on flesh.

This was it, she was really going to do this. With Hot Guy, who she'd only just met officially.

His skin was soft, but the muscles beneath solid, and she smoothed her way up to his shoulders, exploring the sculpted contours of his body. He was so different to Dylan, leaner yet somehow stronger, his physique wasn't gym-puffed-up, it was raw strength, male strength.

He slid his hand down her neck to her chest and caressed her breast through her top.

She tipped her head, welcoming his soft kisses on her neck.

"Condom," he said breathily. "I need to reach a condom."

Condom! Oh fuck! I can't do this.

That one word had made it too real. She was tipsy, reeling from her break-up with Dylan—there was no way should she be doing this with a stranger on her office desk.

"James…I…"

He kissed down her throat, his stubble catching on her skin, all the time continuing to touch her breast. "Mmm…"

"Stop, I…" Oh God. "But…please…"

He held her a little tighter with one arm while with his free hand he appeared to reach for his wallet.

"James, stop, I can't."

He stilled and raised his head. He was breathing fast and his eyes glinted in the darkness.

"I'm sorry, but I just… This is too much, too fast." Damn, she could feel how much he wanted her. But she just couldn't do this. Hell, she'd likely regret stopping this chance of a bit of action in the morning, but one-night stands, rushing into things, that wasn't her style.

"I'm sorry," she said again and slipped her hands from beneath his shirt. She pushed at his chest.

He released her and stood tall. He blew out a long low breath and turned to the window. He took several paces away from her and stopped. Put his hands behind his head, elbows out, and linked his fingers.

She'd ruined it all now, whatever it was they'd started, if indeed it was anything.

Megan stood and adjusted her top, staring at James, who appeared frozen in position.

She felt bad. She'd led him on, got him riled up, given the impression they'd go all the way. "I'm sorry." *God, what am I? A stuck record.*

"No need to apologise," he said, his voice low and grating, as though he was speaking over sandpaper.

"But..."

"It's fine. I'm not in the habit of having sex with women who don't want to have sex with me." He turned and dropped his arms to his sides.

"No, of course not, and I do, want to, it's just—"

"You don't need to explain, Glitter." He glanced at his watch. "Come on. We should go and find you that cab."

6

James

James Carter considered the woman in front of him as she gathered up her purse and what appeared to be a sketchbook and some pencils. Her long dark hair that felt like silk was ruffled from where he'd just fed his fingers through it. Her pretty top was dishevelled and even in the dim light he could tell her cheeks were hot and flushed.

Damn, *she* was hot. He'd been watching her from afar and waiting for the perfect moment to approach. Biding his time until he was in the right mind set—head not bogged down with work—to think about asking a beautiful woman out to dinner. And now he'd gone and blown it. Ruined it all. Why did he have to let lust takeover? Had he no self-control? He was a grown man, for crying out loud.

She stooped and picked up a piece of material.

And wow, the woman could kiss—all soft sweetness laced with the taste of want.

And she *had* wanted it. He knew she had. The way she'd curled her legs around his, explored the flesh on his back, swept her tongue into his mouth. That had been a woman who'd wanted a man, he knew that much about her.

So what the hell had happened?

Had he come on too strong?

No, he couldn't imagine that for a moment. Megan was the sort of woman who oozed sex appeal with every step, every smile and every word she said. But something had stopped her. Something had made her shut down on him.

"Let's go," she said, opening the door.

James grabbed his jacket and moved past the woman who'd stolen his dreams of late.

Once out on the cobbled back street, Megan strode ahead of him. He glanced at the shadows—it wasn't the best place for a woman to walk on her own and he didn't like to think that she did it regularly. And the sound of her heels clicking on the damp stones, they were just an advert to her presence, a flashing beacon that shouted 'vulnerable woman, come and get me'.

And yes, she was vulnerable, not just physically but emotionally too. He watched her hair swishing as she walked, tiny drips of mist making it sparkle. He could see that delicate side of her now, the slice of pain that had gone through her eyes when she'd told him to stop, the stoic way she'd smiled when she'd spoken of her delight at friend's engagement, even though it had clearly struck a painful chord in her.

What happened to her?

"Megan, wait," he called as she turned left at the end of Change Street. Damn it, he'd messed this up so much, she didn't even want to walk next to him. For crying out loud, she was actually running now! He could hear her clipping along the pavement like a bolting pony.

He pushed into a sprint and turned the corner. A cab had pulled up at her side and she climbed in without even a backward glance at him.

"Megan," he said again, quieter, to himself as he came to a halt. "I'm sorry."

The cab navigated into the stream of traffic, the red taillights becoming lost in the sea of cars.

Well, that had been a first—he'd messed up so badly with a woman she'd actually run away from him. He really was losing his touch, his own fault probably, for leaving it so long and working too damn hard. His mastery over the opposite sex had upped and vanished.

"I can't and won't live with that. It's all wrong and not a true portrayal of these peoples' plight, we have to make it real." James was cranky as he worked in the editing suite at Grace Studios. He'd snapped at his colleagues all morning and nothing seemed to be going right. He'd been in London for six months making this documentary and now in the final stages, the pressure to get it right was running high.

"Hey, take a chill pill," Grant said, shaking his head at James.

"Well, it's just..."

"It's fine, it just needs tweaking." Grant frowned. "What's the matter with you today anyway?"

James sighed and rubbed his fingers across his forehead. "Nothing." Well, he was hungry but that wasn't really the problem. Though he would have to feed himself soon, grab something from the canteen.

"Doesn't look like nothing. You can be a grumpy SOB when we're finishing up a project and I know it's all about the fine details, but this takes the damn biscuit."

James reached for his coffee and took a sip. He glanced at the door, wondering how long it would be until the other members of the team came back in.

"What? You gonna tell me or what?" Grant said, sitting back and crossing his arms. "'Cause I'm all ears, mate, and we're all alone. And if you get whatever this is off your chest, you might be a bit easier to put up with for the rest of the day."

James pressed his lips together. If he really thought about it, he could still feel Megan's lips against his, taste her honeyed tongue, feel her soft body pushed into his.

He tried to shove thoughts of last night and having Megan in his arms from his mind.

"It's a woman, isn't it? You've met someone." Grant sat forward, eyes wide, and clapped. "I'll be blowed."

Was it really that obvious? James' scowl deepened.

"So, spill the beans, tell all. What's she like?" Grant folded his arms and nodded. "Come on, I'm curious, you haven't had time for lurve for ages? Not since—"

"It's not love." James tutted. It was far too soon for that word.

"So lust then. Come on, what's her name, where is she from, what's she do?"

"Bloody hell, slow down." James picked up an elastic band from the desk and twirled it around his index finger, pulling it taut so the blood got trapped and made the skin at the tip bright red. "And besides, it was over before it started."

"But you got some, though, right?"

James twisted the elastic around his middle finger, making it as red as the other one.

"What?" Grant held out his palms. "This awful mood and you didn't even get lucky?"

"Shut up, Grant." James tugged the elastic from his fingers and sent it catapult-style across the room so it hit the door square on. "I shouldn't have said anything."

"Doesn't sound like there's much to say." Grant laughed. "Have you lost your touch?"

"Hell no and it wasn't like that." James could feel his already dark mood blackening. "She's just got…issues."

"Like what?"

"Shall we just get this done?" James sat forward and clicked his mouse. He stared at the computer screen. "The sooner the better, and then we can get the hell out of London, it's always bloody raining here, even in the summer. I knew there was a reason I moved to LA."

"Yeah, you're right. Let's get this wrapped up and head home, then we can sort out you getting laid."

James rolled his eyes. Grant might be his best mate, but still, he knew how to push his buttons and wind him up. Plus he wasn't always the most of sophisticated of companions.

But perhaps he was right. He did need to get laid. It had been a long bloody time, which was maybe why his brain hadn't been in control last night.

"So what's her name?"

"Who?" James tapped his toe on the floor, his leather shoe making quick clicking sounds on the hard wood.

"This woman that's got you so on edge."

James wanted to say Glitter, because that's what he called her in his head. But now he knew she had a real name, Megan. And it suited her. It was a pretty name for a pretty lady.

"Well no wonder you didn't get very far," Grant scoffed. "If you didn't even bother to ask her name."

"Of course I did."

"So…what is it?"

"Megan."

"Megan what?"

"I…er…" Damn it. That he didn't know. He recalled telling her his full name but not getting her surname in return. He really was a prat. No wonder last night had gone downhill so rapidly.

"I didn't catch it," James said, sighing. "I guess we started talking about other stuff and it was missed. She runs an up-and-coming shoe design business. Sparkly heels and stuff, really girly." He paused, thinking about her enthusiasm for her business. "And her best friend just got engaged. Although she seemed happy, I got the impression it made her sad, you know?"

"Probably in love with her friend's new fiancé." Grant chuckled. "Doing him on the side."

The hairs on the back of his neck tingled. "No. It wasn't that." He wasn't sure how he was so confident in that statement, but he was. Gut feeling. He just hadn't got that vibe from Megan. There was no hankering after a spoken for man, he'd bet his Rolex on it.

Grant leant forward and concentrated on his screen for a moment, then said, "So what is it that makes this Megan girl sad?"

James shrugged. "I don't know."

"But you'd like to find out?"

Would he? *Yes.*

But he never would. Not now.

"What I'd like to do is get this done and fly back to LA." James nodded at the screen. "I can hear the ocean already."

"Sure thing, boss." Grant moved his mouse around, cropping an image. "I guess it just goes to show London girls aren't for us Californian men."

"Hey, I'm a Londoner, remember."

"Ah yeah. I guess you've just been in the Sunshine State for so long I think of you as one of us."

"Thanks, I think." James rubbed his fingers over his forehead. Eight years of working and living in LA had worn the edges off his homesickness for London, plus the work he'd been doing on documentaries was getting more and more challenging—though rewarding—as his reputation grew. He was being tasked by the studio to create real quality pieces of investigative interest. They were controversial and exposing. The kind of thing he'd hoped to do when studying at King's College.

James loved his job—it took his mind off being single and being away from home. And there was still so much more to tell the world—wrongdoings, injustice, evil to expose—things ordinary people just wouldn't see if it wasn't for directors like him.

But he didn't want to be a bachelor all his life. He had dreams of finding *the one* and enjoying a warm female body in his arms, in his bed, in his life. A string of accolades and reviews didn't warm the sheets at night or satisfy the needs in him.

"What do you think of this clip?" Grant asked, pointing at the screen. It was a woman holding a child. They were stood outside a boarded-up shop and shivering as snow fluttered down on them.

"Play it," James instructed.

Grant did as James had asked. The twenty second shot ran. The woman was talking about cold and hunger. She wore a tatty coat with a frayed collar, a faded headscarf and her cheeks were weather-beaten and red. The child was wrapped in a blanket, presumably because he didn't own a coat, and his eyes held no sparkle, no depth, none of the joy of youth.

"It's powerful," James said, nodding slowly and frowning. "What's the ratio?"

"We have about ten per cent testimonials."

"I think it should stay then, don't you?"

"Yep, I agree." Grant clicked over it, moving it into a 'keep' folder. "At forty-five minutes?"

"Yes, that should do, we can always move it around later." James turned back to his screen. Directing the revealing programme about poverty in inner cities had been harrowing. He hadn't realized there were people living in a country with a welfare system who were so poor they had to choose between heat and food in the winter.

He hoped his documentary, *Poor Choices*, would highlight the issues and encourage the government, charities and the population at large not to turn a blind eye. Not just in the UK, but worldwide. James was passionate about the power of the screen, and using it to do good had become the main focus of his working life.

He set to task on some images for the opening sequence. As he did, his mind went back to Megan again. She was the opposite of the woman with the frayed coat he'd just seen talking. Everything about Megan was polished and perfect. From her soft, flowing hair, to her pretty eyes and fluttery lashes and her bright red, pouty lips that were made for kissing. Her clothes were of the finest material—his palm had slid over her little silky top as he'd enjoyed the feel of her small, fragile body beneath. He'd been able to feel the outline of her bra, satiny and soft, and, if he had to hazard a guess, not at all padded—Megan's petite hourglass shape was all-natural.

Hourglass. Mmm, he would have liked to get a bit more up close and personal with that figure. Maybe she'd be at Frank's Bar again tonight? Perhaps she'd stop in for another glass of wine and to listen to the pianist after she'd spent a long day at her office?

He should go too. It wouldn't exactly be out of his way, or unusual, or as if he were hoping desperately to see her. He stopped at Frank's several nights a week anyway, as it was en route from the studio to his rented apartment.

It had taken him a few weeks of living and working nearby to notice the bar, what with it's blacked-out windows, small sign and no pavement advertising, but once he had, it had become the perfect place to sit when he hadn't fancied going straight back to an empty apartment and eating a meal for one.

Yes, that's what he'd do. He'd stop off, order a beer and sit at the table they'd shared yesterday. Maybe she'd come in, he'd order her a glass of white wine and apologise for his appalling behaviour. Seriously, what had he been thinking?

He vaguely remembered the crash and bang of folders and other stuff falling to the floor as he'd scooped her onto the desk. But it had barely registered. All he'd been thinking about was getting closer to her.

For a few minutes it had been so good, so damn hot… The memory of her letting him slot between her thighs as he'd kissed her and leaned her back on the desk would always be with him.

He clicked onto an image of an empty food cupboard and hoped Grant wouldn't notice his fidgeting.

He pulled in a long, deep breath. It seemed where Glitter—Megan—was concerned, all control went out of the window.

Which was, the more he thought about it, probably the very reason for her running. He'd come on too damn strong, scared the poor soul witless. And that wasn't the type of man he was. He'd always prided himself on sophistication, cool, calm collectiveness. Even if he had been in a bit of a sexual drought lately, that should still be the case.

But this woman had him unravelling at the seams.

His phone bleeped and he glanced at the screen.

"Is that your Megan?" Grant asked, not looking up from what he was doing.

"No, it's Roxy."

"Oh God, really. Now what?" Grant rolled his eyes and shook his head. "Needs collecting from Brighton? Bailing out? Or maybe you need to go and explain to the London Eye that she's very sorry for flashing the lower pods her lacy knickers."

James laughed, but there was little humour there. His young niece had put him through all those things while she'd spent a month completing work experience in London. It had been a joke that she'd wanted to learn about making a documentary, she'd only wanted to party, push the English sense of propriety to the limits and embarrass him as much as she could—or so it seemed.

"No, no trouble," James said, flicking his phone locked and sighing. "She's home, thank goodness. Just landed at LAX and into the arms of her parents again."

"That's a relief."

"You're telling me. That is the last time I agree to let a twenty-year-old hang out with me. Bloody nightmare from start to finish."

"That would sum it up."

"And as if I have time for that kind of crap."

"Who has?"

"Her parents, hopefully, now that she's back under their roof, have all the time in the world for her shenanigans. I pity my sister sometimes, but she was the same at that age so I guess what goes around comes around." He paused. "I wonder what Roxy will tell her boyfriend. Marc, his name is. She called him most days while she was here, spewed a load of shit about what she was learning and how bright her future was going to be because of the London Experience." He made brackets in the air around the last two words. "I can't imagine she'll confess to all the times she spent the night out goodness only knows where. I just got late badly spelt texts telling me not to worry and she'd see me the next day. What was I supposed to do?"

"Nothing you could do. And it's not likely she'll tell this Marc guy anything because what she was learning was how much snakebite and black she could drink, how many vodkas she could guzzle until she fell over and how many English guys' numbers she could collect."

"It did seem that way." James frowned at the memories. "But not my problem anymore. As if I didn't have enough to begin with."

"Yep, one female problem is more than enough at any one time."

James glanced at Grant. "I don't have any now."

"Sure you do?"

"What? Who?"

"Megan, this Megan woman who's gotten under your skin." Grant shook his head. "She is so your problem."

"No she isn't. I'll never see her again."

"Somehow, mate, I think you're wrong there."

7

Megan

"Damn shoe," Megan muttered as she stepped into her office. She glared at the single gold embossed bridal shoe that sat on the top shelf. Yet again it had been the star of an unpleasant dream, no, the star of a nightmare more like...

Fleeing down the aisle had been like wading through treacle, she'd got nowhere fast. Then the glittery heel had caught in a single deep hole and refused to budge. No matter what she'd done—wriggled her foot, pulled her ankle, dragged her nails on the red carpet—she hadn't been able to free herself and get out of the church.

The huge stone walls had closed in on her. The bells had screamed overhead then...then Dylan had walked towards her. His eyes black, as if set only in a skull, and his lips peeled back in a sickening, malicious grin that bared his teeth.

She'd woken again with her heart thudding and her pulse blasting in her ears. The vest top she'd slept in had stuck to her back and her cleavage had been damp with nervous sweat.

The only thing for it had been to jump in a cool shower and drink a cup of strong coffee. But still, as she'd made her way to the office on the Tube, memories of the dream had haunted her. She'd forgotten those long, devil hands that had reached up from the carpet and clawed at her like devils' helpers. And that Dylan's friends had all worn hooded shrouds and cackled at her like witches pleased with their catch.

She shuddered and looked away from the shoe she'd actually walked down the aisle in. It didn't hold good memories.

After pressing the door shut and dropping her keys into her purse, she glanced at her desk.

"Oh shit."

Again her heart rate picked up and a flush of heat travelled over her chest. There was actually very little left on her desk. The shiny wooden surface was clear apart from her laptop and a single sheet of crumpled paper.

Thank goodness her Mac hadn't gone flying. That would have been a major problem.

She rubbed her fingers over her lips and looked at the scatter of files, folders, papers and pencils on the floor. The stapler was spread open as if performing the splits. She'd been so wrapped up in James 'Hot Guy' Carter that she hadn't given a hoot what had upended.

And not surprisingly, because damn, the bloke could kiss. He had the most sensual, pliant lips she'd ever had the pleasure of pressing against hers. And he'd tasted of everything she'd been missing in her life—heat and man, a hint of beer and a whole lot of desire.

"Oh God," she muttered and bent to retrieve the lewd stapler that displayed its insides. She recalled wrapping her legs around his waist, clinging to his hard biceps, offering her neck for his kisses.

A shiver of pleasure rattled up her spine. Oh, the feel of his neat sprinkle of stubble on her throat, the scent of his spiced cologne, the heat of his body seeping into hers.

"Stop it!" Megan gathered up her sketchpad and a sheaf of papers. "It's over now. Before it started."

Of course it was over. She'd behaved like a deer caught in headlights. As soon as it had been a definite they were going to take it further on her desk, she'd put on the brakes and pushed him away.

No, she'd done more than push him away. She'd upped and ran, left the poor bloke standing in the rain as she'd taken off around the corner as fast as she could.

She hadn't even looked back when she'd heard him call her name as she'd jumped into a cab. That couldn't have been a clearer message.

Leave me alone. I'm not interested.

Except she *was* interested. James was hot, yes, but he was also nice. No, nice was the wrong word, it was too passive. He was intelligent, interesting and he had a sparkle in his eye that made her think that he was a person who cared deeply about things he bothered to care about.

For a moment, he'd cared about her.

Or had he just wanted her?

Damn it.

She'd wanted him.

She just hadn't been ready. It was too soon after Dylan.

Wasn't it?

Her phone rang and she glanced at the screen.

Unknown number.

She frowned and hit answer. "Hello."

Nothing.

"Hello?" She pressed the phone harder to her ear, wondering if the reception was dodgy. "Anyone there?"

She could hear a faint sound—traffic?

She ended the call. Whoever it was must be in a bad reception area.

The phone tinkled to life again.

"Hello?"

Quiet. Absolute silence.

"Anyone there?" She frowned at a pile of pencils that lay like a game of chopsticks on the floor, pushed aside in the heat of the moment between her and James.

A shiver went up her spine. "Who is this?"

Nothing.

"Stop calling until you've got reception, I can't hear you." She slid her finger over the screen, scowling as she did so.

It rang again, instantly.

But this time Brendon's smiling face, made up like a cat for last year's Halloween party, filled the screen.

She hit answer. "Hey, you."

"Megan, I—"

"Did you just try and call me?" she asked.

"No, I—"

"Are you sure?"

"Yes, of course, forget that, I'm calling you now." He paused. "And you should kiss me quick and buy me a candyfloss because I am just the bestest best friend ever."

"Well I know that." She smiled and the chilly feeling that had made the hair on the base of her neck tingle waned. Hearing Brendon excited always lifted her mood and made her feel warm and safe. "How are you this morning, Brendon?"

"I am good, more than good, and I have been in full-throttle, full-on Winter Shoes PR mode."

"You have?"

"Yes. I, my pretty, have been up since six wheeling and dealing for you."

"That's very kind but—"

"No time for buts, darling, you have to get your sweet little backside to Grace Studios pronto."

"I do?"

"Yes. I've been helping out with *Ralph and Jayne's* fashion slot, as you know, and today they were supposed to be doing a feature on this season's must-have shoes. Anyways, the shoe woman, Jade Melua or something, has got not only a horrible collection but also a horrible diarrhoea and vomiting bug. Apparently she can't promise not to explode from one end or the other while live on air, so…" He chuckled.

"So…?"

"So, I've told them that I know just the replacement and that you can be here in an hour."

"An hour!"

"Yes, and you will be. The studio is twenty minutes from your office and I know, being the little workaholic that you are, that's where you'll be right this minute."

"Well, yes, but…"

"No buts. All you have to do is grab your boxes of latest on-shelf samples and bring them down here. The girls in the green room will do your hair and makeup, they'll get you camera ready et cetera, et cetera, et cetera."

Megan could just imagine Brendon wafting his hands in the air as he spoke. "And then what?" she asked. "I just hold the shoes to the camera and grin."

"Oh, don't be so ungrateful, you little wench. You know what to do. You chat about the material they're made of, all ethically produced and with your trademark glitter soles. Tell the captivated audience what to wear them with, what occasion, which is every occasion because there is a Winter Shoe for every event in every season." He laughed. "Come on, you'd be nuts to turn this down. People would pay thousands for this kind of advertising and I'm handing it to you on a platter, a goddamn silver platter. There'll be models too, showing them off."

"I'm not turning it down." She straightened her back and glanced around the room, mentally totting up how many samples she had and which would be the best to take.

"Good. I'll see you in twenty, twenty-five minutes at the latest. And just so you know…"

"What?"

"If you don't show up, my darling, my reputation will be in tatters and I'll be useless to you, as a friend and as your PR agent. In fact, I'll be useless to everyone, my life will, officially, be over if I let *Ralph and Jayne* down."

"I'll be there." With her free hand Megan grabbed an enormous holdall from under a chair. "And I'll have everything with me, as long as—"

"Someone does your hair and makeup, yes that's covered. See you soon."

"Yep."

"And, Megan…"

"What?"

"You'll be fabulous, you always are, whatever you do."

Megan rushed through the front doors of Grace Studios with her bag bouncing on her back and the strap looped over her left arm.

"Megan Winter," she said to the stern-looking security guy.

He consulted his clipboard. "Put your bag on there." He indicated a conveyor belt that led to what appeared to be an X-ray machine.

Hurriedly, she dumped her huge bag of stiletto shoes and sandals onto the belt. Hopping from one foot to the other, she watched as it slowly, agonisingly slowly, edged its way towards the black plastic flap.

"I'm in a rush," she said, wringing her hands together.

"Isn't everyone," he replied, nodding seriously.

"Like, I'm supposed to be on air within the hour."

"Isn't everyone," he said again and folded his arms.

The bag disappeared into the machine and he frowned, looking closer at a screen. His thick eyebrows pulled together and he pursed his lips.

What the hell did he think she was, a bloody shoe bomber?

Finally the bag went through the other side, and she dashed through the human security machine. Thankfully it didn't make a sound.

She grabbed her samples, threw the guard a glare then raced towards reception.

"Megan Winter," she said.

"Ah, yes, Brendon Trugate is expecting you." The receptionist picked up a phone and jabbed at a dial with her long red fingernail. "Yes, she's here."

"He's coming?" Megan asked.

"Yes, one minute. Please, take a seat."

Megan was too on edge to take a seat. Instead she paced to a large map of the studio that hung on a wall. It was pale green and the outline of the rooms and the maze of corridors were drawn with golden paint.

She spotted a canteen and licked her lips. She could do with something to eat and drink. She'd dashed out of the house, after her dream, with the intention of grabbing something with the estate agents as a mid-morning snack. But that wasn't going to happen now and her stomach was complaining.

"Megan, you're here. Oh thank the Queen of Sheba for that!"

Megan turned at the sound of Brendon's voice.

"Hey, you." She accepted his flamboyant kisses on her cheeks.

"Now we haven't a moment to lose, chop, chop." He stepped back and clapped. "The girls are waiting and..." He dropped his gaze down her body. "And actually I think that will do. Yes, you will do!"

"What?"

"That outfit. Bravo, darling."

Megan glanced at her sheer stockings, grey pencil skirt and jade silk blouse. It had been a bit of a 'grab and drag on' outfit but it was holding its own. The only thing she'd switched as she'd dashed from her office were her shoes. She'd teamed the look with sparkly green heels that worked with her top's rich tones perfectly.

At least she hadn't been wearing yesterday's jeans and silk top ensemble. That had well and truly been thrown together, admittedly the top was Prada but still, it was on the lowest scale of glam.

But she hadn't dressed to impress that morning. There was no way she'd planned on dropping in at Frank's for a sneaky glass of wine after work.

Was there?

No. Her mind had been muddled, dream-addled. She'd simply pulled on the first thing she'd laid her hands on and dashed out of the door.

Seeing James most certainly hadn't been on her mind.

Though she probably should apologise for running off like that. Disappearing into the mist like some tragic Brontë heroine.

"Oh, for God's sake," she muttered as the emotions of the night before tumbled through her.

"Nope, it's fine." Brendon grabbed her hand. "Come, come, we'll go through your segment while the girls fix this." With his free hand he tugged a lock of her hair that had fallen from the high ponytail she'd dragged it into.

"Thanks, I mean. Yes. I really do need to have a think about what I'm going to say."

"You've got the sales pitch and the brochures memorised, they're in your heart," he said, urging her down a narrow corridor. "Just don't panic."

"I'm not panicking."

They scooted past a variety of doors that held words like *Editing Suite Three, Studio Four, Green Room Nine*.

Megan bit down a bolt of nerves. She'd never done anything like this before. Been on live TV. That wasn't to say she didn't think she couldn't do it, and if it was for her baby, Winter Shoes, she'd do just about anything. But still, even she knew that *Ralph and Jayne* was watched by millions.

"And now, for our weekly fashion advice, we're absolutely thrilled to have Megan Rose Winter on the show." Ralph turned from the camera and grinned at Megan. "Designer, cobbler and all round lovely person."

Megan stretched her lips wide and hoped the smile went to her eyes. She had so much makeup on it made her skin feel heavy, and how the hell did he know she was a lovely person? Before this he'd only said one word to her.

"Hello. Thank you for inviting me." She looked at the camera.

"We're thrilled to have you." Ralph grinned.

"And how long have you been designing shoes?" Jayne asked, tilting her head, an expression of great interest on her face.

"For as long as I can remember," Megan said. "When I was a young girl my friends liked ponies and ballet and I liked drawing, specifically drawing shoes. I liked to use glue and glitter and…" She paused and laughed lightly. "I still do." She held up a deep purple stiletto that had studded straps as well as a sparkling sole.

"Oh yes, now that's pretty," Jayne said, sitting forward and reaching for the shoe. "I'd wear that." She turned it over in her hand and plucked at the straps.

"And you'd look beautiful in them," Megan said, widening her grin so much it hurt her cheeks.

"I'd *feel* beautiful." Jayne nodded and held the shoe towards the camera. "What woman wouldn't? My goodness, even the soles are princess-like." She let out a long low, wistful sigh.

"That is my intention," Megan said, reaching for another shoe. This time a Grecian sandal that had gold diamantés on the buckles and terracotta straps. "To make every woman feel special when they're wearing

Winter Shoes, no matter what else is going on in their life, they know that they can rely on these shoes to make them feel on top of the world."

"And they certainly would in those," Ralph said, indicating a pair of turquoise-coloured towering heels on the sofa beside Megan.

"Yes, I lovingly call these my Empire States," Megan said, smiling. "They are in my range of extra highs, for those girls who like the additional inches."

"Wow they're big." Ralph said. "But I like them."

"It would take a bit of skill to walk in them," Jayne said, smiling and mock-smacking his arm. "You wouldn't be able to, Ralph."

"Damn shame that." Ralph clicked his fingers and tutted in mock disappointment.

Megan kept the grin on her face. This was the type of banter that made *Ralph and Jayne* such a hit with the morning viewing masses. It was corny but still, it was what people wanted, so it seemed.

"So what would you wear these with?" Jayne asked, returning her attention to Megan.

"Well they'd be perfect with jeans."

"No, really?" Jayne looked overly shocked.

"Yes." Megan glanced behind her, hoping to goodness the model would not only appear but also be able to walk in the purple shoes.

An elegant young woman with hair falling to her waist emerged from a red curtain then strutted down a narrow catwalk. She wore tight denims and a purple top that matched Megan's highest shoes.

"Oh my," Jayne said, "who would have thought?"

"Perfect, don't you think? Shoes can brighten an ordinary outfit, make it extraordinary, make you *feel* extraordinary."

The model jutted out her left hip and pouted at the camera.

"How do you feel?" Ralph asked the model.

She looked a little shocked for a moment, as if torn from her modelling into the act of being required to speak. "I, er…extraordinary." She smiled at Megan. "These shoes are high but so wonderfully comfortable."

"Are you sure?" Ralph asked, frowning. "They don't look it." He raised his foot, showing off a flat, black leather shoe.

"Oh yes, I could wear them all day," the model agreed enthusiastically. "The insoles are so soft, padded almost."

Megan could have wrapped the tall, skinny woman in her arms and kissed her. Instead she said seriously, "Yes, I have added extra padding for the balls of the feet. You know what they say? Painful shoes, painful expression. There is just no getting away from sore feet, it shows on your face."

"And in your eyes." Jayne shook her head and tutted. "Heaven knows I've worn some killers."

"Tell me about it." Ralph slapped his hand over his forehead. "I've even had to carry you home a few times."

Jayne giggled.

"And then…" Megan said, as the model disappeared behind the curtain. "For the girls who maybe, you know, have a partner who isn't particularly tall or strong for carrying her home." She glanced at Ralph. She'd show him, she too could ad-lib the way they did. "And don't want to be stumbling, this is how to do glamorous shoes and stay grounded."

Ralph pursed his lips and nodded. His gaze settled on Megan, but it wasn't hostile, it was full of fun, up for banter—he was saying with that look that he approved of her style of presenting. It matched his.

A flush of achievement went through Megan. For a moment she forgot that the camera was there and enjoyed seeing the next model work the runway. Dressed in a neat white dress with a collection of long beaded necklaces, she showcased the Winter Grecian sandals perfectly. Her long, tanned legs couldn't be more ideal for the style.

Thank heavens for Brendon, Megan thought. He was backstage, working his magic and coming up trumps.

"Well I do like those straps." Ralph leant forwards and rested his elbows on his knees. "They're very…"

"Sexy," Megan said then laughed. "That's the idea, to feel and look like you're the star of the show, ready for the red-carpet, the catwalk."

Ralph tore his attention from Megan and looked at the model. "Yes, I can actually see what you mean, what you're going for, they're stunning." His serious expression suddenly lifted and he turned to his wife. "I think I know what I'm getting you for Christmas, my dear."

"What's that?" Jayne shrugged, almost coyly.

"Sexy Winter heels." Ralph chuckled and nodded. "It's a done deal."

8

"Oh, just throw me in a tree and leave me to the owls. You couldn't have been any more fabulous if you'd been Cleopatra lounging in goat's milk."

Megan grinned at Brendon. She was shaking now. As though the end of her segment had suddenly encouraged her adrenal gland to release a glut of hormones to send her skitty. She'd done it—she'd actually gone on camera and spoken to the nation about Winter Shoes. What's more, she'd kept her cool, said everything that had needed to be said and given Ralph Wainwright as good as he'd given.

She'd even enjoyed it. Megan would never have thought that being on the other side of the camera would be her thing, but actually, she'd had a blast.

"You were so natural, just made for this," Brendon said, clasping her hands in his. "I'm so proud, you aced it. I knew you would."

"Thanks." Megan grinned.

"And great products too."

Megan and Brendon turned to the tall model in the Grecian shoes who was slipping out of the white dress.

"I'm glad you think so," Megan said. "I'm passionate about my designs."

"I can tell." The model adjusted the strap on her bra and reached for a pale blue sweater. She appeared completely unselfconscious about standing in just her underwear.

Megan admired her body. She was tall and slim, not like Megan's own shorter, curvier figure. But then she was a model, looking like that was her job.

"Have you got a shop?" the model asked, flicking her hair from the collar of the sweater.

"I'm making most of my sales online, but I have shelf space in a few high-street stores now. Hopefully more soon."

"So if I want a pair of these"—the model held her foot up and nodded at the sandals—"where do I go to get them?"

"It's all on her website." Brendon flapped a Winter Shoes business card in the air. "All purchasing options are on there."

The model took the card and reached for a short denim skirt.

"But you can keep that pair," Megan said, "if they fit okay, which they look as if they do. I'm sorry, I had no idea what size feet the models would have today, I just grabbed what I had and hoped for the best."

"Really?" The model widened her already wide eyes. "Are you sure?"

Brendon coughed, then muttered, "Oh my Lordy."

Megan frowned at him then turned to the model. "Of course, just be sure to tell your friends they're Winter Shoes and direct them to my site."

"I will, thanks." She pulled the skirt up, fastened the button and admired the long-strapped shoes again, which did look stunning on her slender, golden calves. "Really, I appreciate it, Megan, and I hope to see you again."

"Oh you will," Brendon said, wafting his hand in the air. "She's an up-and-coming star this one, talented, beautiful and a natural in front of the camera. Only one place for her to go and that's up, up, up."

Megan felt heat rising on her cheeks. "Brendon…" She ducked her head.

"Well, if you're not going to sing your praises, I will, because you are the designer, and I mean *the* designer to be watching. You mark my words…" He pointed at the model. "Winter Shoes are going to be replacing Wangs and Choos before you know it. Put your Louboutins in the bin, darling, and move those Blahniks, because there's no space in your wardrobe for your *blah*, it's all about the Winter glitter…"

Megan giggled. She hoped what Brendon was saying was true, but she suspected she had a way to go before she could challenge any of the greats he'd just mentioned.

The model smiled and shook her head, managing to look regal as she did so. She grabbed an over-sized Louis Vuitton bag and hoisted it over her shoulder. "I've got to get going, got another shoot this afternoon. Have a good one."

"Thanks," Megan said with a smile. "You too."

"And remember if anyone asks, Winter Shoes, featured on *Ralph and Jayne* this very morning." He pressed a bunch of Megan's business cards into the model's palm. "You might as well be the trendsetter here." He spread out his hands and looked at her feet. "Hey, look, you are. Enjoy it, darling, show it off, be loud and proud."

She gave an amused huff and strode off, crossing her feet over a little with each step as though permanently on a catwalk.

"Holy crock-a-pot," Brendon said, swiping Megan on the arm when she'd gone from earshot. "Seriously?"

"Ow, what?" Megan glared at him.

"Don't give the bloody shoes away. That's profit you're tipping down the drain. You may as well burn your money."

"It's good advertising, besides she was nice."

"Lots of people are nice, are you going to give them all a pair of designer shoes?"

"Well, no…"

He banged his palm on his head. "She would have *bought* a pair, likely by the time she'd reached her next gig they'd have been ordered with the power of her iPhone and dispatched."

"But—"

"No buts, don't give the shoes away, otherwise, well… I may have to quit as your chief PR director." He tutted and tipped his chin.

"Oh." Megan smiled. "Is that your title?"

"Yes, darling, it is, I've decided, and besides you need me, so do as I say when it comes to marketing."

Megan reached for him and pulled him into a hug. "Thanks, for everything. This has been an amazing opportunity and an amazing experience. I don't know what I'd do without you."

Brendon hugged her back, the way he always did, with thin-armed urgency that squeezed air from her lungs.

"It's the least I could do, you've had a rough time lately."

"That's just been made much, much better."

Megan thought of the night before and being in James' arms. He was the opposite of Brendon. His hold had been confident, possessive, appreciative of the female form. His kisses had been laced with desire and his muscles had held harnessed power that had made her quiver with need. And his scent had been rich and masculine, not flowery and soapy the way Brendon's cologne smelt.

"Well let's hope you get tons of sales and more opportunities off the back of this," Brendon said, releasing her and turning to the dressing table. He leaned in to the mirror and checked his hair. "And that those other shops come up trumps with shelf space."

"Yes, that would be great, fingers crossed." Megan watched Brendon as he reached for hairspray and applied fast little squirts to the tips of his hair to keep it just so.

She'd bet her best stockings that James had never applied hairspray in his life. He didn't strike her as a man who had an ounce of vanity or any time for primping and preening. Not that he wasn't drop-dead gorgeous and perfectly presented, it just all seemed natural. The thickness of his dark hair that held a hint of wave had been left to its own devices and luckily it suited him to perfection. His stubble had been neat but dense when she'd seen him and it had made her wonder what it would feel like against her skin, equally when she'd noticed him clean-shaven on the odd occasion she'd have been just as happy to feel that against her cheek too.

Well, at least now she knew what his stubble felt like on her cheek, her neck…

She turned from the mirror. What was she doing? There was no point daydreaming about James Carter. That was one moment that had been and gone. It had a great big tick next to it. Done. Finished before it had started.

And all because she'd been so stupid. All because she'd had a sudden flash of nerves and hadn't been able to keep up with a moment of passion.

Because that's what it had been—raw, blinding passion. They'd admired each other from afar and suddenly, in a blustering whirlwind, had come together. The moment they'd had privacy and been wrapped in desire, there had been nothing to stop them.

Megan had to be honest with herself—it had scared her a little, the intensity in his eyes, the desperation in his voice, the rush of his hands. She'd been with Dylan for so long, the idea of being with another man—at the very last moment before it had happened—had rocked her confidence.

Could I?

Would I?

And what if?

Damn it. Sex was like riding a bike and she was really bloody good at it. She had no reason for a lack of confidence. She was well practiced in all the moves and techniques.

A small tremor went up her spine. She had a feeling James would be well practiced in all the moves and techniques too. He had an air about him that made her think he'd be very good at everything he did, whether it was directing documentaries or making sure a lover was pleased.

"You okay?" Brendon asked, putting down the hairspray.

"Yes, fine."

He turned and frowned. "You look pale."

"I'm just... It's been a full-on morning."

"Have you eaten?"

"No."

He rolled his eyes and shook his head. "Well go, be off with you. There is a canteen just down the hall, go feed yourself before you faint."

"But..."

"No buts, and I can't come with you. I have too much to do here." He sighed dramatically. "That's one segment done but I have to prepare one for *Lunchtime with Lucy*, these must-have summer shawls will not iron themselves."

"Is that really your job?" Megan glanced at a heap of material that she guessed were shawls.

"Everything is my job because it all hinges on my reputation. I'm still freelance here you know, one mistake and poof I could be gone."

"I don't think they could cope without you."

"Very sweet of you to say so, but at the moment, I could do without *you* so *I* can get on. So go feed your poor, neglected stomach and we'll catch up later."

"Okay, and thanks again. For everything."

"I know you'll remember me when you're a multi-millionaire." He grinned as he shook out a shawl.

"Of course I will."

Megan wandered down the hallway, in the direction she'd come in. The scent of the canteen drifted towards her—bacon, coffee, sausages—all the delicious things that made her stomach rumble.

She went into the busy canteen and headed straight for the cooked section. She ordered eggs and toast then watched as they were scooped onto a plate. She grabbed a pot of tea, which she added to her tray, and slid her meal along the metal rails. She wondered if she should add a slice of carrot cake. That would really give her blood sugar a boost and soak up the adrenaline that was still sloshing around her system.

She gasped as her arm bashed into a man to her left. "Oops, sorry." She watched in dismay as a large splash of coffee left his cup and landed on his sleeve. "Oh no," she said, reaching in front of him for a wad of napkins. "I really am sorry…I don't know what happened, I—"

"It's okay, really."

Her heart stuttered—she recognised that voice. She looked up. A fresh shot of adrenaline rushed into her blood stream.

Staring down at her was James Carter. His sensual lips—lips she knew were so damn good at kissing—were slightly parted and his eyebrows were raised. He was clearly as surprised as her.

"Oh," she said, swallowing. "It's you."

"Yes, last time I looked." He appeared to compose himself and took the napkins from her hand. "Maybe next time we meet I'll manage not to get drink thrown on me. It's becoming a habit."

"I…sorry…really, I…"

"Don't worry about it, no point crying over spilt milk, or in this case, spilt coffee."

He dabbed the worst of the liquid from his sweater. She adored his hands, they were big and strong, the nails square and his knuckles wide. There was also just hint of forearm hair that sneaked down over his wrist, barely there but oh, so sexy.

"Can I get you another coffee?" she asked, indicating his cup, which had lost an inch of fluid.

"No, it's fine." He tipped his head. "But you can do something."

"What's that?"

"Join me for lunch, there's a table free by the window." He nodded over her shoulder. "No pianist, though, I'm afraid."

He still wanted to speak to her? Spend time with her? Even after her skittish performance the night before. "Well, er yes, okay. If you want."

"I do." He turned to the cashier who had added up the cost of his lunch. "Shall I?" He looked at her tray.

"No, it's fine, really, I'll get mine."

He paid for his then walked to the table he'd indicated.

Megan watched him go. Damn, he looked hot in those jeans, they were just the right mix of tight and loose. Memories from last night's encounter flooded back to her and she felt the same sense of excitement as she had when they'd been in her office.

"Miss?"

"Mmm..." Megan focused on the cashier. "Oh, sorry."

"Five pounds please."

"Yes. Of course." Megan quickly paid and picked up her tray.

James had taken a seat by the window. He was sipping his coffee.

Megan joined him. She'd hoped he'd look at her with the same admiration she had for him as she sat, but he didn't. Her turning him on then taking flight had clearly put a closed sign on any action happening between them.

Way to go, Megan. First decent man to come your way and you pull down the shutters and ruin it all.

"So, what brings you to Grace Studios?" James asked, biting into a sausage sandwich.

"All a bit last minute, really." Megan poured her tea from a small silvery pot. "*Ralph and Jayne* had a cancellation on a fashion slot and one of the guys on their team is a close friend of mine. He thought of me, bless him, and volunteered my services."

James raised his eyebrows. "So you got to give Winter Shoes a shout out?"

"Yes, amazing right?" She sipped her tea.

"Incredible advertising, money couldn't buy that. *Ralph and Jayne* is watched by half the housewives in the country." He paused. "He must be some friend of yours, this bloke, to do that for you."

"He is. We're really close. I couldn't be without him."

James was silent. He bit into his sandwich again. A flash of darkness went over his eyes as he looked out of the window.

Bloody hell. A flicker of hope warmed Megan's stomach. Was that jealousy? Or if not, was James wondering who this *bloke* was who'd done her such a favour?

If so, maybe all was not lost.

"Brendon, that's his name, my friend." She picked up her knife and fork. "He's unofficially my marketing guru, though I should start paying him really, and he's also one of my biggest fans." She paused. "If he wasn't gay, I'd say he'd be a great catch, but he only has eyes for the men."

"Oh, I see." James nodded and reached for his coffee. "Brendon, you said?"

"Yes, do you know him?" Perhaps he'd seen him about.

"I don't think so."

"He works here a few days a week. On a freelance basis."

"I'm mainly in the editing suite at the moment, we're on the final days of a project." He huffed and his shoulders shifted, stretching his thin sweater between the balls of his biceps. "I only came out here for this because I needed a break from the team."

"Oh?"

"Yes, I always find this last bit stressful, there's so much to cram into such a short space of time and it makes me ache inside to chop bits out that really should be seen." He banged his fist on his chest. "It's important that people see what is going on under their noses and also for a US audience to see the UK isn't all pomp and ceremony."

"It sounds stressful."

"It is." He sighed. "Which is why it's nice to be out of it for ten minutes, at least. And now…now I've seen you too, which makes it all the more pleasant a break."

"I'm glad you think so." Megan glanced away. "After last night."

A silence hung in the air. She shouldn't have brought it up. She should have let sleeping dogs lie and all that.

"Last night," he repeated.

She looked at him again and studied the deep blue flecks in his eyes. "It was just…"

"Too much too soon, for that I apologise sincerely, and I hope you'll forgive me."

"There's nothing to forgive, it takes two to tango." She paused and smiled shyly at her silly analogy. "I shouldn't have…"

"Looked so damn irresistible." He swept his tongue over his bottom lip, leaving a light sheen, and his eyes narrowed slightly.

A tremble went through her. She'd like to explore that sheen, with her own tongue, taste it, add to it, kiss him thoroughly.

"So what do you think?"

"About?" She shifted on her seat and nibbled her bottom lip.

"Tonight, dinner." He placed down his knife and fork and held his hands in the air, palms facing her. "And I'll keep my hands to myself, promise."

He wanted to take her to dinner?

Even after she'd run away without a backward glance?

It seemed he did.

"That would be nice." She nodded. "And…" She wanted to say that he didn't need to keep his hands to himself entirely. She liked his hands, a lot. "And, where are we going?"

"What kind of food do you like?" A smile tugged the right side of his mouth.

"Most things…Italian, Indian."

"I know a great little Italian, I'll book us a table. Eight okay?"

"Yes. That's fine." A tingle shot over her skin. Could today get any better? A great day for Winter Shoes and now a great day for her love life, even when all hope seemed to have been lost.

9

"You're going out with Hot Guy? Like seriously, for real?" Brendon let his jaw hang slack and stared at Megan.

"How the hell did that come about?" Georgie asked, still fiddling with her new ring that they'd all spent the last half an hour admiring and cooing over.

"I just bumped into him."

"Where?" Georgie asked.

"In a canteen."

"And what, you just drooled all over him and he asked you out?" Brendon asked, passing Gucci a chew stick.

"Well, no, I spilt coffee on him actually and—"

"You spilt coffee on him." Brendon snorted. "Cool. Way to go, Megan."

She frowned. "It was an accident."

"So what's his name?" Georgie asked. "I'm guessing he wasn't christened Hot Guy."

Megan flicked the kettle on and reached for three mugs from her cupboard. "James, James Carter."

"Oh, excellent," Brendon said, pulling out his iPhone. "Let's Google him."

"What?" Megan shook her head and pointed the tin of teabags at him. "No, you can't do that. I forbid it."

Brendon gnawed at the inside of his cheek and tapped on his screen.

"Brendon," Megan said. "Don't. Please."

"Too late." He grinned and flashed the phone her way. "James Carter. He's even got his own Wikipedia page." Brendon whistled and studied the screen again. "Born in London thirty-two years ago to Sally and Benjamin Carter. Went to King's College and studied journalism and now an award-winning director."

"Oh, very fancy..." Georgie said, straining her neck to see. "Click on images. I want to see exactly how hot he is."

Brendon fiddled again, then, "Oh, love a duck, Megan Winter, you lucky cow." He swiped his hand over his brow and pretended to swoon. "Georgie Porgy Pudding and Pie, feast your eyes on that!"

"Hell yeah, I approve," Georgie said, smiling. "Not your usual type but well deserving of his Hot Guy title."

"What's my usual type?" Megan asked, glancing at the screen. She couldn't see it properly, though, Brendon was hogging it. But she didn't need to, she was seeing James in the flesh in a few hours' time. And that was so much better than a photograph, because she could smell him too, admire the way he moved, enjoy the way he set his entire concentration on her whenever they were talking.

"Your usual type," Georgie said, frowning. "Well you normally go for tall, blond gym buffs."

"I suppose Dylan was that type."

"Talking of Dylan," Brendon said, "I heard a rumour that he got kicked out of Vogue nightclub last night for being drunk and disorderly." He stooped and picked up Gucci, set him on his lap then tickled him under the neck.

"Why am I not surprised?" Megan said. "Rather than getting leery I much preferred it if he just fell asleep after a belly full but that wasn't often the case." She paused, remembering the times he'd passed out fully dressed. "And that had disadvantages, he snores anyway, but when he's been drinking, my God, it's like an express train in the bedroom."

"Lovely," Georgie said, pulling a face.

"Well, no snoring this time," Brendon said. "He apparently got leery with a member of bar staff when he didn't get served fast enough. He refused to leave when asked by the bouncers so they hauled his ass out of there and left him on the pavement."

Megan winced. How humiliating. She was glad Dylan was nothing to do with her anymore.

"Doesn't sound like drowning his sorrows in alcohol is working out particularly well for him." Georgie stood, went to the fridge then passed Megan the milk.

"Thanks." Megan splashed some into each cup. "I can't help but feel a bit guilty, though. I mean, it was pretty embarrassing what I did to him."

"Hell yeah," Brendon said, nodding. "But you did what you had to do."

"It would have been worse to go through it and then decide you didn't want to be married to him," Georgie said.

"I know, I know." They'd been through this a hundred times, but still, Megan knew that Dylan's erratic behaviour was because of her running out on him in church. If the shoe had been on the other foot and she'd been jilted, she would have felt bloody dreadful.

"And you don't need to feel guilty," Brendon said. "You did him a favour. Who wants to be married to someone who doesn't really love them?"

"I suppose." She paused and poured the tea. "I keep having this weird dream, though."

"Oh, what's that?" Georgie helped herself to a mug and cradled it in her hands.

"It's horrible, I'm running down the aisle, holding my dress, which is really heavy, which it wasn't—it's light as a feather—and I just can't gain speed. It's like I'm running through treacle or something. And then my heel gets stuck, in a weird grate on the carpet, you know, like a vent or something, but I can't really see it because of the dress."

"Then what happens?" Brendon asked, setting Gucci down then also taking a cup of tea.

"I'm pulling my foot, trying to get my shoe off, but I can't. It's stuck on and the shoe is stuck too. I imagine all these horrid Devil hands gripping me, holding me down, like it's the bodies from the graveyard outside reaching upwards for me."

"Ick." Georgie gave a shudder. "You poor thing."

"I know, horrible right?"

"So in your dream you're stuck inside the church?" Brendon asked. "And you can't get out."

"Yes, that's it. And Dylan is coming to get me. Then I wake up, my heart is thumping, I'm sweating, and it takes me a minute to realise that it's only a dream."

"So you've had this more than once?" Georgie asked, looking worried.

"Yes, several times." Megan sipped her tea and shivered. "Nasty, makes me not want to go to sleep. Well, alone anyway."

"So don't." A slow smile spread across Brendon's face. "Go to bed with James Carter. Damn, a night with him would chase away my demons. Oh yes, they'd be running for the hills."

"I'm not going to jump into bed on a first date."

"Sweetpea, sometimes needs must. No one would think badly of you."

"Well I would think badly of me," Megan said. Damn it. She probably should tell her friends about meeting James at Frank's the night before and the scuffle on her office desk. But something held her back.

Was she ashamed? Embarrassed by her skittish behaviour? The sudden lack in confidence?

It all added up to an incident she wanted to put in the past. Lay to rest. Tonight was a new start for her and James, one she hadn't thought she'd be lucky enough to have, so she was going to make the most of it.

"So what are you wearing, for your hot date with Hot Guy?" Georgie asked.

"Not sure yet."

"I wonder where an award-winning director takes his lady friends." Brendon shrugged.

"An Italian restaurant. He asked me what food I liked."

"Oh for goodness' sake, don't order spaghetti, darling," Brendon said with a dramatic sigh. "That's first date rule number one. You might think that scene from *Lady and the Tramp* is cute, but it really isn't when you're a twenty-eight-year-old woman. You'll just look a mess."

Megan laughed. "I won't order spaghetti, I promise, and I'll try not to slurp my food either."

"You should wear that French Connection black dress, the one you wore on your hen night." Georgie nodded. "It's really sexy."

"A bit safe, don't you think?" Brendon frowned. "No, wear that tight pink dress, you know, the one that makes your hips look amazing. He won't be able to resist."

Megan thought for a moment. Wearing jeans and a plain silk top had made her pretty irresistible to James the night before—goodness only knew what wearing that shiny pink dress would do. It hit just above her knee but the neckline plunged so low that leaning forwards in it was an absolute no-no.

A small shiver ran over her shoulders and the nape of her neck. God, the way James had held her, slotted his fingers into her hair and kept her just where he wanted her as he'd kissed her. The memory alone was enough to send heat racing around her body. Would he kiss her like that again?

No. Of course not. She'd ruined any chances of that happening tonight. He'd even said he'd keep his hands to himself. Which of course meant lips and all other parts of his anatomy. She'd be lucky to get a peck on the cheek at the end of her date.

"So, which one are you going for?" Georgie asked.

"I think I'll play it safe and go with the black."

Brendon tutted. "Oh well, have it your way. But at least team it with those glorious red shoes that just came through for next season's collection."

"Mmm, I might." Actually that would look nice. Plus she had a slim belt that matched the shoes and a beautiful purse that would complete the outfit.

"Very elegant," Georgie said, nodding. "Perfect for a date with a gentleman."

"I suppose," Brendon conceded. "This James bloke is, after all, a whole different kettle of fish to Dylan."

"Yes, Dylan liked tighter, shorter, low-cut dresses on me."

"Yet complained if another guy looked at you," Georgie said, finishing her tea and rinsing her cup.

"Yes, he was a bit like that."

"More than a bit. Remember that time we went to Cecconi's and he'd bought you that tiny purple skirt?"

Megan groaned. "Yes, I do. He went mad when the taxi driver wolf-whistled as he drove away."

"And blamed you because you'd sat in the front. He said you'd flashed him."

Megan shook her head and sighed. "He could get so jealous. And there was never any reason for it. I never cheated on him. I've never cheated on anyone—it's just not something I'd do, you both know that."

"Well let's hope James Carter appreciates you for the good and honest woman you are," Georgie said.

"Yes, you're quite a catch, especially after this morning."

"Why, what happened this morning?" Georgie asked.

"Bloody hell." Brendon clapped his hands over his face. "All this admiring of the new ring and the fuss about Megan and Hot Guy going on a date and we forgot to tell you."

"Tell me what?" Georgie looked between Brendon and Megan.

"Our Megan was only the star of the *Ralph and Jayne* show this morning."

"What?" Georgie's mouth hung open.

"You heard right," Brendon said, eyes wide. "There was a last minute fashion opening—God bless nasty doses of diarrhoea and vomiting—that needed filling and I managed to get Winter Shoes a plug."

"Blimey, that's awesome." Georgie looked at Megan. "And you went on? Live TV?"

"Yes, that's how come I was at the studio canteen and bumped into James, literally."

"Ahh…it's making sense now," Georgie said with a nod. "And he was there because he's a hotshot director."

"Exactly."

"Anyways." Brendon flapped his hands. "Our Megan was a hit on the show. Ralph loved her, he said so afterwards."

"He did?" Megan asked.

"Yes, he sought me out, said he's hoping you'll be on the show again."

"That would be great."

"I'm working on it, I'm working on it." Brendon winked. "She really is a natural," he said to Georgie. "Gorgeous, obviously, to look at, but also confident and thinks fast. She kept up with Ralph's ad-lib style of presenting fabulously."

"Do you think?" Megan glowed with the praise.

"Hell yes, he can be a tricky bugger. I've seen him reduce other presenters to tears, not on screen, but afterwards, because he'd made them look stupid. But he likes you, you gave as good as you got and you weren't in awe of him."

"Well I tried."

"Watch this space." He tapped the side of his nose. "I have my fingers in many pies and Winter Shoes is a brand I absolutely believe in."

"And has it made a difference?" Georgie asked. "Any rush in sales this afternoon?"

Megan indicated her laptop. "Yes, it's amazing. I've had a rush of new orders plus re-stocking. I've been hard at it all afternoon and still not finished. I might have to finally take someone else on, to help with the admin side of things."

"Yes, you should, I've been saying that for ages," Georgie said. "It would leave you free for designing and exploring new promotional avenues. You spend too much time on the donkey work that a secretary could do for you."

"Mmm, I know you're right."

"Do you want me to have a look through our files?" Georgie paused. "I know you've been putting it off, but the time has come."

"Yes… Are you allowed to do that, though? Look through the agency files?"

"Sure, that's what they're there for. And I'm certain we'll have someone on the books who you could try out. I'll make sure it's someone decent too. Experienced and efficient."

"I'd appreciate it, thanks." Megan smiled at Georgie. She really was lucky, not only were her best mates excellent at supporting her emotionally, they also came up trumps with practicalities too.

"Well," Brendon said and glanced at his watch. "I must skedaddle, places to go, people to do and all that." He stood and pulled Gucci's lead from his pocket.

Gucci spotted it and ran in tight little circles, yapping loudly.

"What are you up to tonight?" Megan asked.

"I too have a hot date." He tipped his chin in the air and looked smug.

"You have?" Georgie and Megan said together.

"Yes. Don't look so surprised." He frowned and scooped up Gucci to stop his barking.

"It's just you usually would have told us the minute you walked in," Georgie said.

"Well, I didn't want to steal attention from the engagement or Megan's thunder about *Ralph and Jayne*."

"So who is the lucky chap?" Megan asked.

"His name is Seth Walker and I met him at Costa."

"Costa?" Georgie said, raising her eyebrows.

"Yes, you know, the place where they serve coffee."

"Smart arse," Georgie huffed.

"He's a very skilled barista."

"He *works* at Costa?" Megan asked.

"Yes, while he's studying for a degree in sociology. He's a poor student, I said I'd take him for a slap-up meal."

"That's very kind of you."

"I thought so." Brendon scooped up his denim jacket. "Well, also he's going to need some extra calories to burn, because I, unlike Miss Prim-Knickers here"—he gestured to Megan—"*do* put out on first dates, in fact it would be rude not to." He licked his lips and grinned. "Oh yes, I intend for Seth Walker to expend serious amounts of energy later, he's definitely going to need feeding first."

Megan looked around her once again quiet flat. It was good to be back in it and now that her boxes were unpacked and the place was aired and warm, she didn't mind being alone—especially not when she had such a nice evening to look forward to. Plus it was great her friends could just call in on her, they'd stopped doing that when she'd been living with Dylan.

Miss Prim-Knickers! Brendon had a cheek. Just because she wasn't a tart like he was with no shame when it came to adding up the notches on his bedpost. Brendon would happily have a different guy every night of the week—not that he did, even he didn't have the energy for that.

Sometimes Megan worried about him, though. He was, after all, ultimately looking for true love, a person to spend his life with, a man he could trust and invest in the future with. She wasn't sure he'd find it with the one-night stands he seemed to favour. Since she'd known him, he'd only ever had a handful of men who he'd referred to as *boyfriend material* and none of them had ever stuck around for long.

Perhaps he needed a change of scene? A new place to meet people who were interested in more than just instant gratification.

She put the plug in the bath then turned on the taps, pouring in a huge glug of Jo Malone bath foam, for good measure.

Life for Brendon had been hard. He'd never fitted in at school because he was nerdy and sports were not his thing. Once, in a quiet moment, he'd told her he was bullied too and his parents had eventually moved him to a different school. It had solved the problem but meant he'd had long bus journeys to cope with at the start and end of each day.

Megan stripped off her clothes and set them on the wash bin. She glanced at her nails—the pale pink polish wouldn't work with the red and black colour scheme of the evening so she set about removing it.

Perhaps she should have a talk with Brendon. See if this Seth guy could be more. Maybe she'd suggest they all go out for dinner, as a foursome, or a sixsome if Georgie and Tom were up for it too. Yes, that would be good. It might give him the nudge into relationship-land.

Relationship.

Was she ready for another one?

It was all so soon after Dylan. She hadn't imagined that she'd go on a date for months, yet here she was, already going out for dinner with someone.

But it didn't feel like she'd only just met James. She'd been admiring him for ages. And it seemed he had her too.

She dropped the cotton wool in the bin and turned off the tap.

He'd said he'd fantasised about her. Thought about kissing her, touching her... What else had he imagined?

She dipped her toe into the water to test the temperature. Satisfied, she climbed in and let the warmth surround her. She rested back and let out a long sigh as the bubbles wafted around her chin.

If she was honest, she'd thought about him too. She'd tried not to, it had felt unfaithful to Dylan, but a girl could look, or so she'd told herself. And not looking at James when she'd seen him at Frank's Bar—whether it was seeing him slipping in from the safety of her office or actually studying him as she sipped her wine—had been impossible.

She swooshed the water over her arms and watched the bubbles popping and shifting against her skin. She had a pleasant feeling of anticipation in her stomach. The evening was going to be good, she could tell. James was so considerate making sure they were going to a restaurant where she'd like the menu. Dylan had loved carvery meals and all-you-can-eat buffets. Not really her thing, but she'd been dragged along to them often enough to get used to them. The thought of an elegant Italian with a handsome man was definitely something worth looking forward to.

Thank goodness for second chances.

She got out the bath and dried off. Her skin was hot and tingly but the heat had made her thirsty so she pulled on a fluffy white dressing gown and headed into the kitchen.

As she filled a tumbler from the tap, a figure marching down the path towards her apartment caught her attention.

Georgie.

What was she doing back so soon? They'd only said goodbye an hour ago.

Her lightweight mac was flapping furiously, her hair whipping out behind her and there was a flush of colour on her cheeks.

"What the…?"

Megan knocked back a few mouthfuls of water then rushed to the door. She pulled it open and within seconds Georgie was in front of her. Now she was closer, Megan could see that her red cheeks were tear-stained and her eyes puffy.

"What on earth is the matter?" Megan said, pulling her friend close for a hug. So many things were going through her mind. Had someone been hurt? Was Tom okay?

"He's so unreasonable. I just don't understand why he has to do it?" Georgie hung on to Megan and sobbed.

"Do what?" Megan was alarmed. She'd never seen Georgie so upset and so angry at the same time. "Are you talking about Tom?"

"Yes." Georgie released her. She stepped into Megan's apartment and through to the living room, her fists clenched at her sides. Once there she paced to the window, the kitchen then back towards the sofa.

Megan watched her agitated movements from the doorway. "What's he done?"

"He's only gone and started planning a bloody stag weekend to Amsterdam, hasn't he."

"Oh..." She paused. "And Amsterdam is a problem because...?"

"Of course it's a problem." Georgie pushed her hands through her hair and actually stomped one of her feet on the carpet. "Here was me thinking we'd have a nice spa day, me, you, and Brendon, something elegant and relaxing, and he's off with not one or two, but ten mates to the sex capital of Europe."

"But they'll just be drinking and having a laugh, I'm sure nothing—"

"A weekend of drinking, smoking and chasing women...!"

"Tom wouldn't—"

"But the temptation will be there. I know Tom loves me but he's still a man and his mates, especially that Ed and Neil, they'll be window shopping for...you know...and egging all the others on. I can just imagine them now, wandering down those seedy backstreets..."

"Tom wouldn't though...I know he wouldn't." Megan would bet her last pound on it. Tom was devoted, loyal and very much in love with Georgie. Why would he risk anything?

The fight seemed to go from Georgie. She studied Megan then sat heavily on the couch. "I know. You're right. It's just..."

Megan sat next to her and draped an arm over her shoulder, pulling her close. "It just seems unfair, is that what you mean?" she asked softly, then pressed a kiss to Georgie's hair.

"Yes, and he didn't think to ask me first what I thought. That's what hurts the most. He's just started organising it with his mates."

"I guess that's something that takes a while to get used to when you get married, always having to think of another person as well as yourself. Ask before you plan things to make sure it works for you both."

Georgie was quiet for a moment. "I suppose." She spread out the fingers on her left hand. The gem in her new ring caught the light.

"It really is beautiful," Megan said, rubbing her finger on the back of Georgie's hand. "And he chose that all by himself. He didn't ask you first about that, did he?"

"No, I guess not."

"And he got it right."

Georgie sighed.

"You'll just have to trust him on this one too."

"Maybe you're right." She fiddled with the ring. "I love it. Really love it."

"And you love him and he loves you, so it will all be okay."

Georgie released a juddering little sob, emotions clearly bubbling up inside of her. "Can I stay here tonight? I don't want to be alone in my flat."

Megan hesitated for a brief moment. "Of course."

"You sure?"

"Yes, we'll find a girly movie and order in pizza. In fact, I've got *Notting Hill* down there on DVD, been meaning to watch it for ages, I love that film."

Georgie had clearly forgotten about Megan's plans to go out with James.

"Me too. Hugh is great in that film." Georgie wiped at her cheeks. "Can I borrow some pyjamas?" She looked at Megan's dressing gown. "Then we can slob out together, no men allowed. Push them from our minds for a few blissful hours."

"Of course, I've got plenty."

Georgie managed a shaky smile.

Megan thought of James and her heart sank. She'd have to explain very quietly at the door when he came to collect her that she couldn't go. He'd be disappointed, as was she, but Georgie was her priority. She'd never known her and Tom to argue to the point Georgie stormed away in tears. And it was her, Megan, she'd come to, which of course was how it should be and she wouldn't have it any other way. "I'll go get you some. I have some new pink fleece ones, really cosy."

"Thank you, Megan. You're the best, you know that."

"And you're the best too, my *best* friend." She peeled away a lock of Georgie's hair that was stuck to her hot cheek. "It will be all right, you know."

"I hope so."

"It will be. You'll see."

As Megan was rooting around in her drawer for the new pyjamas she heard Georgie's phone ring, then her voice. It sounded a little heated and she wondered if it was Tom calling to talk things through. If so, she wasn't sure what his chances were of winning Georgie round tonight.

"Here you go," Megan mouthed, wandering back into the living room and setting down the clothes.

"You're where?" Georgie said into the phone. She frowned at Megan as though not understanding the conversation she was having. "What window?" She paused and sniffed. "Oh, okay."

Georgie walked to Megan's big window then let out a squeal.

Megan rushed to see what she was looking at.

Tom stood at the end of the path. Looking tall and handsome in jeans and a tight grey T-shirt. He held a huge bunch of red roses and a big bit of card that had the word *sorry* written on it in marker pen. He was holding both things in one hand and in the other his phone that was pressed to his ear.

"Tom!" Georgie shouted. "You're here?"

Megan couldn't hear his reply but she could see his mouth moving as he stared at them both.

"Yes, I'm coming, now. Okay." Georgie flicked off her phone and turned to Megan. "I won't be needing the pyjamas now. Tom is taking me out. He's sorry, he's said we'll talk about it and he'll change the whole trip if I really can't cope."

"See," Megan said, smiling and her heart lifting. "It will all be okay because you love each other."

"We do, very much." She gave Megan a final hug then dashed from the room, the front door banged behind her.

Megan watched as Georgie ran down the path and flung her arms around Tom's neck. He swirled her around, his face also full of emotion.

Yes, Megan, thought, they really would be all right, more than all right, they'd be just perfect.

10

"You look…stunning," James said, his gaze slipping down Megan's body.

"What, this old thing?" She brushed an invisible speck of dust from her dress and shifted from one foot to the other.

He mock huffed. "I don't think *old* or *thing* are suitable words for that dress."

Megan flushed a little at his approving expression then absorbed the sight of him. He looked so big standing on her doorstep, and his dark suit fitted him to perfection. He didn't wear a tie and the top button of his pale blue shirt was undone, revealing just a tiny hint of bronzed skin. A sudden memory of the night before flitted through her mind. Her, pulling his shirt from his waistband, smoothing her hands over the soft flesh on his back, grabbing his wide shoulders, dragging him closer, wanting more…

"I will, er…just get my purse. Hang on." She rushed into the flat, tugged the kitchen window shut then collected her purse and keys.

Damn, I should have invited him in.

No, the place was too messy. She'd spent so long doing her hair and nails, fussing over makeup and applying her red lipstick that she hadn't got around to tidying. The kitchen was littered with plates and mugs, she had laundry drying on the radiator in the living area—including underwear—and Gucci had left hair on the sofa that needed to be hoovered up.

She pulled in a deep breath, tipped her chin then walked as calmly as she could down the hallway. James was studying her with that oh-so-serious expression of his—the one that pulled his eyebrows low and set his mouth in a straight line that was as sexy as hell.

She wondered what his hopes were for the evening.

Dinner and fun conversation, or more…?

And if he did want more, would she commit to it this time, or would she run?

"I've got the car," he said.

"Oh, that's good." She pulled her door shut and locked it. "Is it far then, to the restaurant?"

"Not really." He led the way down the steps and into the evening sunlight. "It's back over near Change Street. I'm sorry if you've just made that journey."

"No, I worked from home this afternoon."

James pointed a set of keys at a shiny black Volvo and it beeped and flashed to life. He opened the passenger door and held it wide. "There you go."

"Thank you." Megan smiled and sat inside the car. How chivalrous. She couldn't remember the last time a man had opened a door for her.

James carefully shut it and walked around the front of the car. His jacket flapped a little in the breeze and he pushed his fingers through his hair. The way he moved was easy and confident, fluid.

He sat in the driver's seat and started the engine.

Megan could smell him now that they were in an enclosed space. The same delicious cologne he'd had on yesterday but a little stronger, as though it had been applied more recently and wasn't lingering from a morning application. She licked her lips and fastened her seatbelt. "Did you have a busy afternoon at the studio?"

"Yes." He indicated and pulled into the traffic. "But we got a lot done. Grant, that's my assistant director, he's a trooper, really great at slicing final segments together. I'd be lost without him."

"I'm thinking of getting an assistant."

"Are you?" He glanced at her then turned back to the road.

"Yes. My friend Georgie works in HR, for an agency, she's going to sort me someone out, just to try and see how I get on."

"How *you* get on?" He slid up the gears. "Does that mean you're worrying about letting some of your control of Winter Shoes go to someone else?"

Am I?

Megan hadn't really thought about it. But now that she had, it probably was the real reason she'd been stalling getting help. Winter Shoes was her baby—she knew everything about it. Had a handle on every email, call and sale. "It will feel a bit strange, letting another person get on board."

"But after this morning, all that promotion, it's likely you'll need it. Sales may well take off."

"I'm already seeing that, which is great."

He turned and flashed her a smile. "Wonderful news."

She shrugged. "Well, it's not like I'm saving the world or curing cancer but you know, everyone needs shoes and girls like pretty ones."

"I think guys like seeing girls in pretty shoes." He glanced at her red heels. "So you're doing a great service."

"Thank you. It's important to feel that your days are spent doing something worthwhile, don't you think?"

"I couldn't agree more. I've directed a ton of different genre documentaries for Grace Studios, some I've loved, some I've hated."

"And the ones you've loved, why have you enjoyed them?"

"Because they've all made me feel like I'm making a difference. Doing something good for someone, or for a group of people. Even if it's just spotlighting a cause."

"Like what?" Megan was intrigued. He was clearly very good at his job if he'd won awards, but she wasn't supposed to know about his achievements. She'd die if he found out Brendon had Googled him. How immature was that.

"A couple of years ago I travelled to Afghanistan and followed a group of surgeons who had given up their own time to volunteer at Camp Bastion."

"That sounds dangerous."

He half shrugged. "Not really, not if we stayed on camp."

"And did you?"

"Most of the time."

"But you went out some of the time?" Megan felt alarmed at the thought of James walking where landmines were buried and snipers hid in the hills. "Where people get shot and blown up?"

"It was necessary for making the documentary. It wasn't a soft, cuddly programme for kids—it was to show people sitting at home on their comfy sofas sipping tea what was going on out there." He turned left and slowed as he drove down a narrower street.

"And what was going on out there?"

A frown tugged at his forehead. "A lot of brutality. What those guys are risking for our freedom is breathtakingly selfless. Many of them pay the ultimate price."

Megan was quiet. She'd seen enough sadness on the news to know what had been happening in the Middle East, but seeing it first-hand, the way James had, that must have been be harrowing.

"How long were you there for?"

"Two months the first time."

"You went back?"

"Yes, we made another documentary about weapon malfunction. But we were only there three weeks for that one." He shook his head and pulled into a parking space. "Made me rather unpopular with a few ammunition companies."

"And was that a problem?"

"Not for me." He smiled. "Here we are."

Megan turned. They were outside a small restaurant called Bettino's. It was housed in an old Tudor building with black beams, white paintwork and with wrought-iron railings separating it from the pavement. "It looks nice."

"It is." James turned off the engine and got out of the car.

Megan was just about to open her door but he beat her to it.

"Thank you," she said again.

He held his hand out for her to take.

His palm was warm and steady as she stepped onto the pavement, and a fizz of sensation tickled up her arm.

If just one small touch makes me feel like that…?

He shut the door and placed his hand on the small of her back. "Come on. I'll introduce you to Rosseta."

"Rosseta?"

"Yes, she's the owner and a friend too." He pushed open the door.

Instantly the seductive scents of basil and thyme, garlic and sweet onions filled her nose. Her stomach rumbled and she realised it had been hours since she'd eaten.

"Ah, *bella*, my James, here you are." An older woman, short and slightly hunched, bustled forward, her arms outstretched.

"Rosseta, how are you?" James smiled and kissed her on both cheeks.

The scarf she had wrapped around her head jiggled as she moved and when she smiled a row of creases concertinaed on her cheeks and around her eyes.

"I am good, better for seeing you here," she said then looked at Megan. "And finally you have brought a beautiful lady with you. Ah, *bella, molto bella*." She clasped her hands beneath her chin and nodded approvingly.

Megan fidgeted with her purse and smiled. "Thank you."

"Rosseta's beef lasagne is to die for," James said. "I fear since I've been living in London I may have eaten my entire body weight in it."

Rosseta laughed. "But that is good. You are a big man. You need food, and Italian food is the best. Better than all the rest."

"I agree," James said.

"Come, come this way." She crooked her finger. "I have you the best table. The very best."

"Thank you." James indicated for Megan to follow Rosseta.

They went up a slim set of steps, several of which were wonky, and emerged onto a small balcony area that had half a dozen tables set on it. Each was dressed in pristine white linen and had a single red rose in a slim vase in the centre. Candles were set about, their flames shivering gently and casting shadows up the walls. Two tables were already occupied by couples talking quietly and sipping wine.

"Here," Rosseta said, pulling a chair out from the farthest table. It was set in a slight recess, away from the others and provided both privacy and a nice view of the restaurant, as well as out onto the street.

"Thank you." Megan sat and placed her purse on her lap.

"You would like champagne, yes?" Rosseta looked at James expectantly.

"If that's what Megan would like," he said.

Megan smiled. Oh, she was getting spoilt. "That sounds lovely."

"Then yes, a bottle please, and is it okay if I leave the car out the front overnight?"

"Of course, of course. I will keep close eye on it for you." She narrowed her eyes and glanced outside.

James smiled and sat.

Rosseta bustled off.

"We'll use a cab," James said. "I fancy a glass or two of champagne. It's not every day of the week I get such lovely company for dinner."

"You're very kind."

"I'm honest." He poured two glasses of water from a jug that held lemon slices and ice cubes. "And just so I don't worry if you've arrived home safely, the cab will drop you off at your place, then me back near here. I'll feel better that way."

"That's not necessary."

"I insist."

"Well, thank you very much." She didn't want to think about the end of the evening. They'd only just arrived. Only just started their date. Besides, the thought of more than a cab ride home at the end of the night was growing more and more appealing as she looked at James.

The guy was hot.

Seriously hot!

He shrugged out of his jacket and hung it over the back of his chair. His short-sleeved shirt had a faint chequered pattern on it and when he folded his arms it tightened around his biceps. She wondered what he'd worn in Afghanistan—if he'd dressed like the military did in desert camouflage combats, and if he'd needed to wear bulletproof vests and a helmet.

The thought of him needing that protection sent a shiver through her. The thought of anything hurting him made her feel queasy.

She took a sip of water.

"Here you are." Rosseta appeared with two champagne flutes and a bottle of Moët & Chandon in an ice bucket.

"Thanks." James sat back and watched as she poured the frothy liquid.

"Would you like menu?" Rosseta asked.

"Not for me, I'll go with the lasagne." He smiled. "Why don't you try it, Megan?"

"Now I've heard such glowing praises I'm curious." She smiled. "So yes, please."

"Only if you want to," James said.

"Yes, it's perfect. I love lasagne."

"You will love this one. And it will put meat on your bones." Rosseta nodded seriously and put the champagne bottle in the bucket. "I will bring bread and olives now."

"She must think I'm skinny," Megan said when Rosseta was out of earshot.

"She's always trying to fatten everyone up. I suspect that's why the lasagne is so good. It's full of cream and butter." He paused and settled his steady attention on her. "And for the record, I think you're perfect and you shouldn't change a thing."

Megan bit on her bottom lip and glanced away. The look in his eyes. It could make a girl strip off there and then and demand to be taken. Being around James was dangerous if she intended to keep her clothes on tonight.

"I'm sorry," he said. "Clearly where you're concerned I can't help myself and I just say and do whatever comes to mind."

"No, don't apologise. It's nice… You're nice."

He smiled. "Well thank you. Nice is a good start."

Now she felt silly. *Nice.* He was more than nice, he was drop-dead gorgeous. But she wouldn't tell him that. She might show him, one day, but she wouldn't say it.

"Cheers." He picked up his drink and touched the rim of it to hers. "Here's to good Italian food."

"And dates. It's been a long time since I've been on one." She smiled and sipped her drink.

"Why is that?" he asked. "I would have thought you'd be inundated with offers."

"No, I've been busy setting up Winter Shoes." And planning a wedding, which she'd run from as fast as her legs would carry her, but James didn't need to know that she was a jilter. Not yet anyway. It wasn't her proudest moment.

"I know what you mean. I haven't exactly had time to date either."

"I can't imagine there's anywhere to go for fancy candlelit meals in a war zone."

He nodded. "You're right there. Plus here in London, I've been so busy with this latest project. I've found it's taken up a lot of brain space, and when I get like that I'm just so…"

"Focused?"

"Yes, that's the word. Focused. It's all I think about, day and night. I've got to get it done and get it done right. It's consuming."

"Because you're a perfectionist."

"Yes."

"It's a trait that is both a blessing and a curse. I'm like that with my shoes, they have to be perfect of course, but then there is the box, the after service, the website, the branding and marketing. If any of it isn't absolutely spot-on, I just can't rest."

"Which is what makes it a successful business. But it can be exhausting being a perfectionist."

"Exactly. Sometimes, if I add up the hours I've worked in a week, I shock myself."

"Well in that case you do need an assistant. And the sooner the better."

"Yes. I'm going to make it a priority. Get another desk and chair in my office, computer too, and delegate some of the more mundane tasks."

He nodded and pressed his lips together.

Megan wondered if he was thinking about her desk. How he'd lifted her onto it the night before and kissed her.

"Here we are, my young lovers." Rosseta set down a basket of bread and a terracotta bowl full of dark green olives.

Lovers.

Megan glanced away.

They so nearly had been.

They still might be.

Her stomach did a roll of excitement and she was aware of her heart thudding in her chest. "So what," she said, reaching for a piece of bread and hoping her cheeks hadn't flushed, "is next on the agenda for you? You said you'd nearly finished this project."

"Yes, shouldn't be much longer on it, only a matter of days. Then I'll go back to the studios, hopefully take a bit of a break if there is nothing I need to fill in for then start on something new."

"Do you know what yet?"

"Not exactly but I have a few ideas. I have to submit them to the board with all the details, approximate delivery time, cost and all that, and see if they go for it."

"Not Afghanistan again?"

"No." He shook his head. "Not Afghanistan."

Megan couldn't help a sigh of relief. She knew these programmes were important and had to be made, but not by James. Not by her James.

Her James.

Where the hell had that come from?

"I'd like to do some work in Central America, there are some fierce drug cartels there that make life miserable for the local population. The governments don't do anything to help, but they would if pressure was put on them by the US."

"That sounds dangerous."

He smiled and ate an olive. When he'd swallowed he said, "Yes, I imagine it will have some risks involved. Neither the government or the drug barons would take kindly to having their illegal activities exposed to the rest of the world."

"But you would do it anyway."

"Yes. I would do it anyway."

She frowned.

He chuckled. "But don't panic. It's just a thought, a seed of an idea. It will probably never happen—nine out of ten proposals get turned down by the board because they're either too expensive or too risky."

"Well this one sounds far too risky. I'm sure your family would be worried sick."

"There's just Mum left now, Dad passed five years ago."

"Oh, I'm sorry."

"Thank you, but she's fine. Happy playing bridge in Oxford with her friends and doting on one of my sister's two kids."

"That sounds nice."

"It is, they're four and two, a handful but adorable. My other sister lives in America, she's Roxy's mum, as you know. What about you, Megan? Have you got family nearby?"

She pulled in a deep breath. This was a question she'd dreaded. "No, they live in Sydney."

"Wow, that's a long way off."

"It is."

"But you don't have an Australian accent."

"Well no, I've only been there once." She smiled. "They emigrated a few years ago. Dad had a great opportunity, the last big promotion before retirement and they jumped at the chance. I could have gone too, but I had a life here, thoughts of setting up my own business, friends, you know…"

"Still, that must have been hard, saying goodbye."

"Horrendous to be honest, but I put a brave face on it." The turmoil of emotions had set her nerves on edge for weeks. She'd been happy and excited for them but she'd been the one, after all, being left behind. For a while she'd grieved for them, the ache in her chest a constant dark ache that had stalked her.

"Do you regret not going too?"

"Sometimes, especially when I see my sister getting taller. She's turning from a teen to a young woman and I'm not there with her."

"Oh, how old is she?"

"Seventeen and loving the Aussie life. Spends her days at the beach and cooking on the barbeque. Still hassles me to send her shoes every season, though, which of course I do because I'm a soft touch." Megan smiled at the thought of Olivia, her sunny personality and her pretty face. Australia suited her down to the ground.

"When are you seeing them next? Any plans?"

"Hopefully by the end of the year. Perhaps I'll plan a trip for Christmas, enjoy singing *Jingle Bells* and *Silent Night* in a bikini on the beach."

"Sounds fun." He smiled.

"Indeed." Megan sat back as a steaming lasagne was placed in front of her

"What do you think of this then?" James asked, shaking out his napkin.

"It looks amazing." And it did. Still bubbling and with masses of melted cheese, the meal filled her plate to almost overflowing. "Huge."

He picked up his knife and fork. "Just have as much as you fancy."

11

Megan glanced outside. It was dark now. All the lights were on in the restaurant and the candles gave the place a cosy, seductive glow. The champagne had made her relax as had the easy, flowing conversation with James, and now, with a delicious, fluffy chocolate mousse to enjoy, she was feeling very content.

"This is amazing," she said, sliding the spoon from her mouth and savouring the rich flavour.

James watched her and licked a spot of cream from his own lips. "So is this." He indicated the bowl in front of him. "Would you like to try it?"

"Please..." She looked at his tiramisu, which appeared incredibly decadent.

He loaded his spoon with a section from the end he hadn't started and held it over the table, avoiding knocking over the red rose and the candle that sat between them.

Megan opened her mouth and studied the concentration on his face as he gently fed her the morsel of dessert.

The coffee flavours burst on her tongue and the cream slipped over her palate. She spread the soft textured treat around her mouth and sighed. "Mmm..."

"Good, eh?" he said, smiling and nodding.

"Very." Now she was torn. She should have ordered that.

Next time.

Next time? Would there be a next time? She hoped so. She wanted to see James again. He was charming yet also at ease with himself, which in turn made her feel comfortable. There was no tension, no worrying if she'd say or do the wrong thing as there had been with Dylan. Plus James gave her the feeling that he was genuinely interested in her. That what she said mattered to him.

Not that she wished to talk about herself. Her curiosity had always been piqued by James Carter—Hot Guy—right from the first moment she'd seen him. Now she needed to know more, to find out everything about him. Not only that, as he spoke she found herself staring at his beautiful mouth, at the hint of stubble that sat over his top lip and jawline, the small mole on his cheek and the tiny lines at the edges of his eyes that deepened when he smiled.

She shifted on her seat. *Oh, that mouth.* Now he was talking about a movie his friend had worked on that was up for an Oscar. She was impressed with what he was saying but her thoughts kept wandering to last night and having that mouth on her.

A flutter of excitement trickled over her body as a tumble of memories flashed through her mind. She wished she hadn't run from him but she had and she couldn't rewind time. However, perhaps she could make up for it—tonight.

"Would you like anything else?" James asked.

Megan glanced at her empty bowl. "No, thanks, that was lovely."

"Coffee?"

She looked at him and tipped her head.

The candlelight danced on his face, highlighting the strong angle of his jaw and his straight nose.

"Coffee would be nice." She paused. "But not here."

"Oh?" He raised his eyebrows.

"Maybe back at yours." God, when had she got so forward? "You said you don't live far…from here."

Surprise flashed over his face. "I don't, it's just around the corner."

Had he presumed that coffee meant sex? Was he that kind of man? Or would he take her at her word—coffee, nothing else?

She guessed she'd have to wait and see. But one thing was for sure, her nerves of last night felt like a distant memory—the feel of James' body against hers was one she wanted to make reality again.

"Well, that would be a nice end to the evening." She placed her purse on the table and smiled. "If it's really not far."

"It isn't, and I agree, a nice way to end to the evening." He held her gaze for a moment then gestured to a passing waiter. "The bill, please."

"Certainly, Mr Carter."

"Tea, would be better," Megan said. "Coffee will keep me awake all night."

He nodded. "I can do tea for you. Wouldn't want you up all night when you have a busy day tomorrow."

"Thank you." But she did want to stay up some of the night. With him.

The waiter appeared with the bill.

"Shall we—?"

"Absolutely not," he said firmly.

She frowned. "Are you sure?" She and Dylan had always gone halves. It was how he'd liked to do it, so their outings were fair, he'd said.

"I asked you out for dinner." James placed several notes on the tiny silver tray. "I want to pay."

"Well thank you. It's very kind of you and it was amazing food."

"You're welcome and I'm glad you enjoyed it. And there was nothing kind about it, I wanted your company."

He stood and waited as she placed her napkin on the table and brushed a few crumbs from her lap.

Megan stood.

"We'll walk to mine, if you're okay to do that?" He glanced at her high heels.

"Of course. It's a warm night."

James bid goodbye to Rosseta, and they stepped out into the pleasant evening. The stars shone and a gentle breeze blew warm air from the south. He held out the crook of his arm for her to take.

Megan slipped her hand into the 'V' of his elbow and breathed in the night. The streets were quiet, the lamp posts haloed in the night air, and the scent of summer lingered—hot tarmac, sun lotion and car fumes.

"This way," James said, heading deeper into the quiet, narrow street Bettino's was set on.

The click of Megan's heels on the pavement was the only sound for several minutes. She spotted a cat watching them from a garden wall, and overhead, a cloud crossed the moon, darkening their way momentarily.

"Here we are," James said, fishing in his pocket for his keys.

Megan looked at the house they'd stopped at. It was an old Victorian-style terrace with a large bay window and a generous porch. Over the green door was a section of stained glass and there appeared to be at least two bedrooms upstairs and an attic room.

"It's only rented," James said, opening the door and flicking on a hall light. "I didn't fancy staying in a hotel for several months as we made this documentary so it seemed like the best option."

"It's nice." Megan stepped in. It was warmer than outside and smelt faintly of James' aftershave.

"It does the job." He shut the door and set his keys on the hall table. They tinkled on the wood. "This way. I'll put the kettle on." He took off his jacket and rested it on the newel.

Megan set her purse down next to his keys and followed him through a lounge that had a low, burgundy leather couch and a log-burning stove set beneath an ornate mantel. The wooden floor had a large oriental-style rug set over it, and a big mirror hung above the fireplace.

She stopped at the kitchen door and watched as James moved around, putting on the kettle, grabbing mugs, teabags then milk from the fridge. He looked big in the small space and damn, his suit trousers fitted him nicely.

"It's got a bit of a garden," James said, nodding at a dark window that looked out over the back of the house. "Not that I've used it much while I've been here."

"Too busy."

"Exactly." He smiled. "Sugar?"

"No, just milk."

He passed her a cup of tea. "Here you go."

"Thanks."

He picked up his own cup and moved past her to the lounge area. As he did so his arm brushed hers.

The tickle of his skin against Megan's sent heat through her. She wanted more than just a brief connection. She wanted to get better acquainted with James' skin, and not just on his arms.

She followed him and sat on the sofa as he shut the curtains then put on some low music.

He flicked on a lamp to add to the ambience, the light from which spread a buttery glow over the room.

"Thank you for taking me to Bettino's," she said then sipped her tea. "It's always nice to find these out of the way little restaurants that offer great food."

"Maybe you'll come again with me?" He placed his drink on the table and sat next to her. Close, but not so they were touching.

"I'd like that."

They were silent for a moment.

"Megan, I—" He shook his head.

"What?" A knot of worry curled in Megan's belly. He looked anxious and a line had formed between his eyebrows.

He shook his head a little. "I really am sorry about last night, you know, in your office. You must think I'm terribly uncouth."

Phew, it was only that which had made him look so worried.

"I don't think that at all." She set her cup down. "Though I'm sure *you* must think that I'm a terrible tease."

He huffed. "Tease, no. Gorgeous, yes. You can't help it if you make a guy want you."

He wants me?

Megan looked into his eyes, they sparkled in the low lighting and his pupils were large. "Do you *still* want me?"

He was silent. His lips held in a tight line.

Oh, God. She'd ruined it all. So what was this then? Dinner and now here… What was the point if he didn't want her? "James?"

"I do," he said, "but I understand you don't want me, or—"

"I never said that."

He smiled, just a little, tiny twitches in the corners of his mouth. "Well I understand that you're not the type of woman to just have a bit of fun with." He reached for her hand. "You're special, Megan, and I wish I'd put a bit more finesse into seducing you instead of going for it all gung-ho."

Seducing me?

The way he talked, looked at her. It created a longing in her soul that she'd never felt before.

"So how would you have…?" She paused and swallowed. "Seduced me if you'd put more finesse into it?"

He tipped his head. "You really want to know?"

"Yes." A flush of anticipation spread over her body, spiking the hairs on the back of her neck. "I do."

He took her hand and rested it between his. "It would have started off with a romantic candlelit meal in a really nice restaurant."

"It would?"

"Yes, somewhere intimate, great food, somewhere I could buy you champagne and feed you sweet treats from my spoon."

"Oh…" She nodded and looked down at her hand pressed between his. The sensation of being held by him like that was both thrilling and sensual.

"I'd spend time getting to know you, enjoying watching you speak, smile, laugh." He paused and leaned a little closer.

Megan could feel his body heat now. His shoulder was just touching hers. She swiped her tongue over her bottom lip. "And what else would you do?"

"And then I'd hope, at the end of the evening, when I dropped you home that perhaps I'd be able to steal a kiss."

"A kiss," she whispered.

"Yes, just a kiss, nothing more, that would be enough to make me feel like I'd won an Oscar." He moved closer still, his nose now only an inch from hers. "And then I'd ask you out again, hope that you'd say yes and I'd perhaps be lucky enough to kiss you again. Maybe hold you in my arms too."

"I think…that sounds perfect."

"You do?"

"Yes, all of it." Megan rested her free hand on his shoulder and felt the hardness of his body beneath. "Especially the kissing part."

"I'm glad you think so."

She could smell him and feel his breath on her cheek.

"I think, maybe…" she said. "You should show me this kiss."

He released her hand and tucked a strand of hair behind her ear. "Are you sure?"

"Yes…"

He cupped her jaw and pressed his lips over hers.

Megan sighed into the kiss, loving being reminded of just how good he was with his mouth. He peeked his tongue between her lips, swept it over the tip of hers, all the time holding her face in a gentle but possessive hold.

Megan adored the feeling of being surrounded by him. He was firm yet tender, controlling yet gentle.

"Damn, you taste so good," he said, his lips moving against hers as he spoke.

"You *feel* good," she answered, running her hand down to his elbow, taking in the contours of his biceps, then back up again. She slid her hand further and rested it against his neck, his pulse beating against her palm, strong and steady but a little quick.

"Megan, I…" He shifted on the seat.

She smiled at him and reached for the top button on his shirt. Instead of rushing frantically, this time she slowly undid it, then the next and the next.

James sat very still, watching her intently, almost as if he was afraid she might run off into the night at any moment if he broke the spell.

But Megan was going nowhere. As she undid each button, another few inches of his flesh was revealed. Sun-kissed flesh that was stretched over taut muscles. She reached his navel, tugged the shirt from the waistband of his trousers.

"Megan," he murmured, reaching for both her wrists and wrapping his big fingers around them.

"Yes?" She stilled. His hold was tight.

"Do you want to take this upstairs…to bed?"

Her heart was beating fast. She ached to be touched more by him, feel skin-on-skin contact, have him close and closer still. "Yes." She nodded. "That's what I want."

He kissed her again, holding her wrists for a moment before wrapping his arms around her.

She sagged against him, pressing herself to his chest. This was better than their frantic tryst on the desk, this was more about savouring the moment, enjoying each other… There was no rush.

They had all night.

Eventually James broke the kiss and stood. He held out his hand. "Come on, this way."

She took his hand and followed him from the lounge and into the hallway. She was a little apprehensive, but not nervous—she was sure she was doing the right thing, and she'd been able to think of little else for hours.

He walked up the stairs, and she stayed close, holding his hand tightly. They went into the first room on the left, which was in darkness except for a faint glow through the drawn curtains from the moonlight.

Megan let her eyes focus for a few seconds then made out a large bed—white duvet neat and straight—in the centre of the room, and a dressing table and wardrobe against the wall.

James pulled off his undone shirt and laid it over a straight-backed chair.

Megan toed off her shoes and let her feet sink into the soft carpet. As he came to stand next to her she became aware of how much shorter than him she was.

"You're beautiful," he said, smoothing his hand along her arm.

"Thank you," she whispered. Her breaths were a little fast. He was beautiful too, his torso muscular and chiselled.

He smiled, just a little, then kissed her again, his tongue curling with hers. He took hold of the zip at the back of her dress and drew it down.

The material loosened around Megan's body. Her stomach was a tight knot of longing.

The sound of the zipper was loud for a moment then stopped when he'd undone the dress. Very gently he placed his hands on her shoulders, over the slim straps, then pushed them wide.

The dress slid over her chest, hips and pooled on the floor, its silky lining speeding its journey.

James pulled back and looked at her. "Heaven help me," he muttered thickly.

The adoration in his voice washed over Megan and by his words she guessed he liked the black balcony bra and lacy thong she was wearing. She reached up and touched his hair, stroking a strand that had fallen onto his forehead. They were so close, one small move from her and they'd be kissing again.

He slipped his finger beneath her bra strap, swept it downward, tickling over her flesh.

Megan pressed her lips to his face, just to the right of his mouth and let his stubble scratch lightly against her.

He continued to explore her, sweeping his finger between her skin and her underwear.

A shiver went over Megan, lust and need building within her.

"You okay?" he asked, his lips now at her ear.

"Yes..." Her voice was breathy.

He held her close, unhooked her bra and let it fall to the floor. They kissed, exploring each other's mouth and tangling tongues.

He was hot and hard all over. His pecs were wide and his arms thick and strong.

We fit so well.

Dark desire shot through Megan. Thoughts of Dylan and Winter Shoes were a million miles away. There was only James—her and James and all the delights that were to come.

He steered her to the bed and eased her down, his body hovering over her.

She ran her hand up his back and arched her neck, allowing him to explore her throat with his tongue as he swept his hands over her chest. He combined light pinches with delicate strokes setting her body on fire.

"James..." she murmured as he drifted lower, as if he were learning her shape, worshipping her soft curves.

"I..."

"Enjoy," he whispered, kissing her hip. "I know I will."

She'd been self-conscious in the past doing this, with a new lover, but not James, he made it all feel so right, so perfect.

She slid one hand into his hair, fisted the sheet with the other and bit down on her lip. He was building up the pressure. Her pulse thudded in her ears and her belly tightened.

"Oh God..." she groaned.

"Condom," he muttered, suddenly reaching to the left and fumbling in a drawer.

"Yes..." she gasped, moving more fully onto the bed. Oh, she'd been so close, she still was. Megan held on to his shoulders and stared at the dark lust flashing in his eyes.

For a moment it was as if they were in slow motion as they connected so perfectly.

She held her breath and willed her muscles to relax.

"I don't think...I'm going to have much stamina," James said, his voice hoarse. "You feel too damn good."

"I'm...nearly...there." She gripped the back of his neck and pulled him close for a deep kiss.

As he dropped over her their connection deepened. He began to rock, with long, steady thrusts that pushed the air from her lungs.

Megan broke the kiss, unable to concentrate now that the coil of pleasure inside her was on the verge of release.

James was panting, his chest rubbing against her.

"Yes, yes..." she said, then groaned again. "Don't stop." What he was doing felt so good.

James framed her face with his hands and stared down into her eyes.

Beneath Megan's hands, his muscles turned to granite. "James," she gasped, dragging her nails over his shoulders.

He sought her mouth and kissed her.

Her breaths were hard to catch and her whole body felt electrified. It had been so long since she'd been with anyone other than Dylan, but James was so in tune with her, they were like two pieces of a jigsaw coming together.

She stroked over the place she'd just scratched then down his back. His skin was a little damp with sweat.

"You okay?" he asked by her ear, his breathing loud.

"Yes, never better."

"That was amazing..." He nibbled on her lobe. "*You're* amazing."

12

James

James woke to the sound of the birds that roosted in the skinny tree by his window. The room was warm and he felt utterly relaxed and at peace with the world. For a moment, unlike every other day, he kept his eyes closed and enjoyed the feeling of having a woman in his bed and in his arms.

Megan's legs were tangled with his—so slim and soft—and her palm rested over his heart. He breathed deeply, relishing the fruity shampoo scent of her hair.

When had he last appreciated the company of a hot woman? He was embarrassed to admit he couldn't recall the length of time it had been, though he did know it had been with Jenny, his ex who was now honeymooning in Bali.

Not that he'd minded being alone these last few years. It was the way he was wired—he was self-sufficient, independent, focused, but then…well, when the choice of company was as pretty and sweet, as endearing and entertaining as Megan, it seemed foolish to be trapped in his self-imposed solitary confinement. Being alone was over-rated, or so he'd just reminded himself.

He stroked the back of his thumb over her bare shoulder, admiring the porcelain delicateness of her skin. Everything about Megan was perfect. Her quick smile, her intelligent eyes, her gorgeous body with curves that were enough to make him want to throw everything away and make her his. He didn't know what it was about her that brought out the Neanderthal in him but thoughts of throwing her over his shoulder and claiming her for all of time kept barging into his consciousness.

It was almost instinctual.

And damn, that sexy black underwear he'd discovered last night when her dress had landed on the floor. If he'd known she'd been wearing that while they'd been in the restaurant, he would have sat there imagining it the entire evening.

As it was, the black lace had sapped his stamina when he'd come face-to-face with it. Megan was a stunning woman but wrapped up in beautiful lingerie, she'd been all his fantasies come true.

He brushed over her forearm and circled her wrist with his fingers. She was so tiny and fine-boned. That alone brought out his protective streak. He wanted to bang his chest and tell the world she was his, keep everyone else away and ensure nothing bad ever happened to her.

Which was of course a continuation of his ridiculous thinking. Who was he? Tarzan? And why would she need protecting?

She did occasionally get a dart of sadness in her eyes, though, and he couldn't put his finger on why.

Perhaps it was simply her family living in Australia? Was she lonely? They'd moved to the other side of the world and left her here. Her own choice yes, but choosing between going with her family or staying was always going to be hard, no matter what the final decision.

But maybe it was more. Perhaps there was something else that gave her the haunted, distant expression he'd seen her wearing at Frank's as she'd nursed a glass of wine in the evenings, spinning the stem and frowning into the pale golden liquid as though her thoughts were a million miles away.

She stirred a little, moved her legs and sighed softly.

He held her closer, enjoying the way her warm chest was pressing into his. She was so responsive, all of her, that it had been almost effortless because they'd been perfectly in synch, their bodies in time. He adored her all the more for that, for being so giving and relaxed.

He licked his lips, recalling her taste.

The clock showed eight—it was well past his usual time to be at the studio. Grant would no doubt be wondering where he was. He could hardly say he was getting some from the pretty girl he'd met at Frank's Bar. Grant would have a field day ribbing him about it and asking for information.

Information James didn't want to give. This was all so new and special. It was just for them, Megan and him. It was almost as if their new fledgling relationship was made of glass—the thinnest, most delicate glass imaginable. And even someone else knowing about it, talking about them, might cause it to shatter. He didn't want the bubble to burst.

He held her tighter still, knowing that soon he'd have to get out of bed and shower. Much as he'd like to wake her with a morning session, he didn't think they were quite at that stage yet, and with Megan, it was too special to risk spooking her. Maybe a few dates down the road—if he was lucky enough to have her agree to spend more time with him—he'd wake her that way and get her day started with one hell of a bang.

And his too.

Her breathing was deep and slow, she was clearly not about to wake. He wondered if she was late for something but then recalled her saying that she was just in her office all day and making it a priority to find an assistant.

Damn, he hoped he could see her again, preferably that night. They had to make the most of his time in London. Would she enjoy the theatre? He thought she might. His friend worked at the box office at the Apollo—maybe he should take her there? Then afterwards for drinks at The Ritz, that would be special and fun.

He smoothed his hand over her shoulder, beneath the duvet and onto the first rise of her hip.

God, her body was flawless. Whether she was in sexy tight jeans, a figure-hugging dress, seriously sexy underwear or naked, it all worked for him.

It was no good. He'd have to get into a cold shower.

Very carefully he unwound himself from her, resting her arm on a pillow where his body had been and pulling the duvet up to her neck to keep her warm.

For a moment he stared down at her. She looked good in his bed—dark hair fanning her face, sultry lips parted a fraction and limbs and hips creating gentle hills beneath the duvet.

Maybe he should shower then make her breakfast in bed. There were long-stemmed red flowers in the back garden, the same red as her sexy lipstick. He'd pick one to put on the tray and show her his romantic side.

Yep, that's what he'd do.

He crept from the room and shut the door with a quiet click. There was pineapple juice in the fridge, and he'd bought croissants yesterday—he could warm a couple in the oven.

Then after breakfast, perhaps, if she were as willing, he'd crawl into bed with her again for a repeat performance of last night. Grant would just have to cope. It was only wrapping up, he'd done it a million times—he could hold the fort until James rolled out of bed.

He yanked on the shower tap and switched it to cold. "Damn it," he muttered, stepping beneath the flow. Luckily the icy water dampened down his desire.

He reached for the shampoo and scrubbed at his hair, rinsing in the chilly spray. Then he covered himself with shower gel and created a lather. Megan smelt so sweet all over, he reckoned she must use fruity soap.

Damn it, now he was fantasising and remembering the night before. He was never going to get control of himself if memories kept besieging him like this.

He pressed his palms to the shower wall and let the water beat down on his shoulders. He took several deep breaths and went through a mental list of all the things he needed to achieve at the studio that day.

Grant would be slicing and adding segments together right now. Then when he arrived and sat next to him—in the dull, quiet, unsexy studio—he needed to finalise the last piece of music and also double, triple check the end credits. If they missed someone out there'd be hell to pay.

He sucked in a breath then blew it out, water spraying from his mouth. That was it, he was okay. Control had returned.

He stepped out of the shower and wrapped a towel around his waist. Grabbed another and scrubbed it over his hair. He added a slick of deodorant, brushed his teeth then pulled on a pair of sweats that had been hanging over the bath—they would do for now, save reaching into his wardrobe and risk disturbing Megan.

He tiptoed down the stairs, avoiding two that he knew creaked, and went into the kitchen. After flicking on the oven to heat the croissants, he filled the kettle.

The weather was glorious and he flung open the back door to the warm morning. Stepping out to pick a flower, James found himself humming—not something he was prone to doing—and he smiled as he selected a perfect rose. Megan would like this one, it was also the colour of her gorgeous lipstick and those glittery shoes she'd worn last night.

Soon he had a tray set with croissants, a small pot of jam, tea, juice, the flower and even a neatly folded napkin.

He went up the stairs, not avoiding the creaking ones and hoping the tea wouldn't slosh over the side of the cup. He pushed open the bedroom door with his foot and stepped inside. "Good morning, sleepy head."

He stopped. Froze. Stared at the empty bed.

She wasn't there. He frowned and looked over his shoulder. Perhaps she was in the bathroom.

No. The door was wide open, the way he'd left it ten minutes ago.

He set the tray on the dressing table and glanced around. Her shoes were gone, as was her dress and the underwear he'd had to step over to get out of the room for his shower.

"Fuck it." He scowled.

Surely she wouldn't have? Who did that? Who the hell spent a fantastic bloody night with someone then just vanished into thin air the next morning?

He stared at the dent in the bed, the shape their joined bodies had made and the hollow in the pillow from her head.

She wouldn't have.

She was probably in the lounge and he just hadn't seen her as he'd walked past so intent on the tea not spilling.

"Megan?" James picked up the tray again. "Megan, I've made you breakfast."

He retraced his steps and headed back into the lounge, hoping to see her sitting on the sofa, tapping on her phone or applying lipstick.

But no.

The room was empty.

He paused and swallowed. A build-up of bile attacked his gullet and stung like a bee.

After abandoning the tray on the coffee table, he went back into the hall, knowing this time he'd see what he should have noticed minutes earlier when he'd taken the breakfast upstairs.

Her purse was gone.

"Jesus," he muttered, shoving his fingers through his damp hair. "She really has just vanished. What the hell is the matter with this woman?"

A battle of anger, frustration and concern warred within him. What was going on? Last night she'd been the one to suggest coming back to his place after the meal. She'd been the one who'd started undressing him, who'd pulled him close, closer still. Why run? Why vanish?

He opened the front door and glanced left and right, looking up and down the street, knowing he wouldn't see her but hoping he might.

Of course he didn't.

Well, she couldn't just disappear. Not really, he knew where she lived, where she worked.

Damn it.

Was he really that awful to be around? He was a bit out of practice in the bedroom department but once you could do it, well…you could do it. And she certainly hadn't complained, in fact she'd convinced him of the opposite—she'd had a great a time, the same as he had.

He shut the door and paced to the kitchen. He flicked the kettle back on to make coffee. He needed it, and the stronger the better.

One hour later, James was in the studio working on the final credits. He was tense, on edge, there were knots in his shoulders that had wrapped around his nerves and were stabbing at him like hot needles.

"Got a face like a long weekend, you have," Grant muttered.

"What?" James frowned at the screen and clicked the mouse so hard he wondered for a moment if he'd broken it.

"You, what the hell has rattled your cage?" Grant tutted. "You march in here two hours late, don't say hello to anyone and drink coffee as though the planet is going to run out of the stuff tomorrow."

"Nothing has…rattled my cage. I just want to get this done and dusted."

"It will be soon enough. Not much more to get through."

"Huh, well the sooner I'm back in bloody LA the better."

"It's that woman again, isn't it?"

"No." James dragged in a deep breath and held it for a few seconds. His heart did a couple of annoyingly fast beats.

"It is, I can tell. I haven't been your best buddy for all these years and not learnt to tell when you're lying about a chick."

"Why would I lie?" His frown deepened.

"I don't know but you are. You always pull that face and hold your breath when you're about to lie."

"I do not." James turned to Grant, irritation rapidly morphing to anger and flooding his veins with heat. Damn it, his shoulders hurt. "And I do not lie, either."

"Whatever. Now come on, what happened?" Grant glanced around the empty studio. "Quick, tell, before the others come back."

James rubbed his fingers over his temple, wishing he could erase the scowl that seemed permanently etched there since he'd discovered Megan had run off. Unfortunately Grant knew him too damn well and could read him like a book.

"A problem shared is a problem halved," Grant said in a sing-song voice.

James rolled his eyes.

"Come on, I'm being serious." Grant's expression changed to one of concern. "What's up, buddy?"

Oh what the hell.

"I took her out, last night, to Bettino's."

"That nice Italian near you?" Grant nodded approvingly.

"Yeah, that's the one."

"*Oh, la, la.* Very romantic."

"It was, perfect in fact. She, I mean we, had a nice time. Great food, fine wine, easy conversation over candlelight."

"And then what…?"

"And then she suggested we go back to mine, you know, for coffee."

"She was up for it then, unlike the time before." Grant grinned a little manically and rubbed his hands together.

James didn't want to disclose anything about Megan and what they'd done in bed—that they'd even been to bed together. It didn't seem tasteful and not at all gentlemanly. It was like breaking a confidence of hers.

"So what's the problem?" Grant frowned. "Oh no, don't tell me you've been celibate for so long you've forgotten your moves." He made a lewd rocking motion with his hips.

"No." James turned back to the screen. "Everything is in full working order thank you very much and…"

"What?" Grant asked. "Spill the beans."

"It was pretty damn amazing if you must know. More than amazing, we were good together, you know…"

"So, why the long face?"

James sighed. He'd said more than he wanted to now. It made him feel like a schoolboy discussing conquests behind the bike shed.

"What?" Grant said, pressing the matter. "What is it?"

"Persistent bugger, aren't you?"

"I am where you're concerned, James. If you're screwed up over some London chick, this editing won't get done and I won't get home. And believe you me, I want to get home and soon."

"Fair enough." James shrugged. "She just disappeared, like, in the morning. I got up, showered, went downstairs. One minute she was there, the next, vanished."

"She did a runner?"

"Not even a goodbye or a note. Just…gone."

"Why?"

"I don't bloody know, do I?" If only he did.

"But it's hacked you off big time?"

"Yes, wouldn't it you?"

"Hell yeah." Grant nodded and his eyes widened. "It seriously would."

"So you see why I'm not all rainbows and bloody fairy dust this morning."

Grant huffed. "As if you ever are."

James sighed and turned back to the screen. Telling Grant hadn't halved his problem at all. Now he just felt even more stupid. Gullible, in fact. Twice now, Megan had just upped and run from him.

What was her problem?

One thing was for sure, he didn't make investigative documentaries because he wasn't bothered about finding answers. And Megan of Winter Shoes had filled his mind with questions that he *would* resolve. If it was the last thing he did, he'd find out why she kept taking off and leaving him feeling like the biggest loser in town.

13

Megan

Megan placed her palms over her face and groaned. "Just shoot me now."

"Pull your silly self together." Brendon rested his arm around her shoulder and gave her a gentle squeeze. "It'll be all right. Worse things happen in space."

"How can it be all right?" Megan sank deeper into her sofa. She wanted it to just swallow her up, like a big cushioned mouth, and keep her in the dark and the warm where no one could see her, or hear her or wonder at her stupidity. "I just upped and ran…again."

"Again?" Brendon placed Gucci on the floor then pulled Megan's forearms so she had no choice but to look at him. "What do you mean *again*?"

"Well, we…er…"

"Spill, spill…"

Oh, the shame of it. Twice she'd bolted like a scared deer. James would think she was pathetic and immature at best, messed up in the head at worst.

"In the canteen, at the studio." She paused. She might as well fess up to Brendon—he'd get it out of her eventually. "That wasn't the first time I got chatting to James Carter."

Brendon's lips parted and he looked stunned. He quickly recovered. "So when? When did you officially *meet* Hot Guy?"

"The night before, at Frank's."

"The night our Georgie got engaged?"

"Yes. I was supposed to be meeting her, you know, for a quick glass of wine, and she called, all excited, and told me her news." Megan smiled at the memory. Georgie's voice had been a pitch higher and her words had tumbled over themselves. "And naturally she was otherwise occupied so she skipped our meeting. James came over to me, I don't know why when I've sat there on my own so many times but that night he asked if he could join me."

"And of course you said yes – Gucci, stop that, stop that… Sorry, he's always had a thing for your cat doorstop."

"I've noticed."

Gucci was curled over the black and white sandbag that was shaped like a cat and his furry little body was humping wildly.

"He'll get bored in a minute." Brendon tutted. "I thought dogs were supposed to hate cats."

"Well he likes that one."

"So what happened then?" Brendon asked, dismissing Gucci's behaviour with a flick of his wrist. "Tell me, tell me. Did you just up and run from Frank's? Oh, those cobbles darling, what shoes were you wearing? You'll have wrecked them."

"My Morocco ones, but they're okay." She stared at the blank TV screen. She could see her and Brendon's reflection in the blackness. "We went to my office. He walked me there." A shudder skittered down her back.

"What? Is he a revolting kisser or something?" Brendon appeared aghast at the thought.

"No, no, he's a wonderful kisser, so gentle yet firm, you know…"

"Mmm…" Brendon's expression softened. "Masterful yet tender. Dominant but sensitive."

"Yes, that's it but I hadn't wanted to walk out on my own, that street can be a bit creepy at night. It's dark and full of echoes and goodness knows what's happened there over the centuries."

"What like Jack the Ripper and stuff?"

"Yes." She paused. "When I went into the bar I had this weird feeling, like I was being watched or something, from the shadows."

"Well you were, by Hot Guy." Brendon rolled his eyes. "Obviously."

"No, he wasn't there then, and it wasn't a nice being-admired feeling, it made the hairs on my arms stand up and gave me goosebumps." Megan rubbed her forearms, her skin tingling at the memory. "There was someone or something there, I'm sure of it."

"Bloody hell. You need to chillax, girl. Your imagination is running riot. Come on, this requires yoga."

"What?"

"You still got that yoga DVD I bought you for Christmas?"

"Yes, it's on the shelf." Megan pointed to a collection of disks.

"Great, come on." He scanned her outfit—sweats and a T-shirt and bare feet. "You'll do."

"But I've never done yoga."

"Which is exactly why I bought you this. You need to get in touch with your zen. Connect your yin and yang, feed your spirit and your soul with goodness."

"And I can do that by contorting myself into a downward dog?"

"Yes, and by breathing, letting out all of that tension. And while we're doing it"—he flicked on the TV and shoved in *The Tranquility Zone: Part One*—"you can tell me exactly what happened with Hot Guy in your office and exactly why you ran away after a night of perfectly fine sex."

"It was more than fine."

"I can well believe it, lucky thing you." He winked then dropped to the ground and crossed his legs in front of himself. "Come here." He patted the floor.

Gucci ran over to the spot he'd indicated and sat, his little pink tongue hanging out and his tail wagging.

"Okay, this side," Brendon said, tapping the opposite side to Gucci. "That spot's claimed."

Megan sighed then did as he'd asked. Dreamy music filled the room and a skinny woman in a purple tracksuit started talking about breathing from the base of the abdomen to the tips of shoulders.

"Hey, anyone in?"

"In here, Georgie," Megan called.

"You really should lock your door, Megan. There's nutters out there. They could just wander in." Brendon shook his head and paused the DVD.

"Hey, are you calling me a nutter?" Georgie said, appearing in the doorway. She dropped her handbag and sweater on the couch.

"You said it." Brendon grinned.

"This was in your letterbox." Georgie held up an envelope. It had *Megan* typed on the front. "Hand delivered, by the looks of it."

"Thanks, I'll open it after this."

"What are you doing?" Georgie tipped her head and studied them sitting on the floor.

"Yoga," Brendon said. "It's the only way Megan can cope with telling us about the date with Hot Guy." He rolled his eyes. "She's freaking out. She messed up…but it's okay, we just need the facts, that's all. Then we can decide on her best course of action."

"Hey, I am here, you know." Megan frowned and crossed her legs the way she used to when sitting at school as a child.

"Yes, for now…Runner."

"Bloody hell, what happened?" Georgie sat too, facing the TV and with her legs crossed in the same way as Megan and Brendon.

"Take deep breaths, Megan," Brendon said, "from your core, each rib expanding and contracting, and I'll fill Georgie in."

"There's not much to say—" Megan started.

"Breathe, with your fingers like this, make them open and close." He placed his hands on his lower ribs and breathed in deep, his fingers splaying as his chest expanded.

Megan copied.

"So she went out," he said, turning to Georgie. "Beautiful food, candles, great conversation and then went back to his place for a bit of how's your father."

"Oh, Megan, back in the saddle then." Georgie winked at her.

Megan's frown deepened. "Don't. I'm already wishing I hadn't jumped into bed with him on a first date. He'll think I'm easy."

"I don't think so, it wasn't a first date," Brendon said, hitting play again on the TV but keeping the sound on mute. "Come on, everyone into cobra."

"What?" Megan said.

"Now, it's good for you. Chop, chop."

Megan and Georgie shared a look then lay on their stomachs the way Brendon was with their backs curved into a 'C' shape and their arms locked in front of them.

"What do you mean?" Megan said. "It wasn't a first date?"

"Well..." Brendon said, fluttering his eyes shut. "You had wine at Frank's and then lunch at the studio. Technically, it was a third date."

"You did? You had wine?" Georgie looked surprised but quickly went on, "Well third date is perfectly acceptable. I bonked Tom something stupid on our third date and that didn't put him off."

"Really?" Megan asked.

"Yeah, at that hotel in Brighton, remember?"

"Oh yes, that's the one I was at a few weeks ago." Brendon let out a long, low sigh as though many memories were coming back. "Big beds and enormous showers with all these little jets coming out of the wall and—"

"So tell me about the wine?" Georgie cut him off before he gave too much information as he was prone to doing about hot nights. "At Frank's?"

"It wasn't planned, we just got talking over a drink," Megan said. "And it led to a kiss and...I guess Brendon is right. We're getting to know each other."

"So what happened last night?" Georgie asked. "Why the emergency yoga?"

"Come on, downward dog." Brendon nodded at the screen. The purple tracksuit lady had her bum in the air and her hands and feet on the floor. Her long blonde ponytail lay like a coiled snake on her mat.

"Was he crap?" Georgie asked, manoeuvring into position. "Small...?"

"No..." Megan said, staring at her knees. "Nothing like that. It was perfect, he was great and very well..."

"What?" Brendon and Georgie said together. "But what?"

Megan sighed and felt the blood rush to her cheeks. "I had that dream again, you know, the one where I'm running down the aisle and my heel gets stuck. I get stuck. It's horrible, panic sweeps through me. These disgusting hands from the graveyard are trying to pull me down into the darkness. No matter how hard I struggle I can't get away and Dylan is there. He's coming towards me, hand outstretched. He wants me, to keep, for all of time. I hate the look in his eyes, he's furious at me for running."

She paused and went onto her tiptoes the way Brendon was. The stretch in the backs of her thighs was nice—she was a little achy from her bedroom athletics the night before. "And then at the worst point of the dream, when Dylan grabs me and I have to choose between going underground into Hell or going with Dylan, I woke. For a moment I didn't know where I was, that the dream had ended. I didn't recognise the room, you know what it's like, a bit disorientating when you wake up somewhere new, somewhere you haven't seen in daylight."

"Mmm, yep, happened many a time," Brendon said, kicking his left leg out behind him and narrowly missing Gucci, who was weaving between them.

"And then of course I remembered. The whole night came flashing back. James and me and what we'd done and I just felt...so...like it was too soon, you know, after Dylan."

"But it felt right?" Georgie said, copying Brendon and back-swinging her leg.

"It did feel right." Megan sighed. "Very right. And with hindsight I wish I'd stayed, talked to him, gone into the kitchen where he was. But my heart was going like the clappers, the dream was so fresh in my head. I was claustrophobic, I was…"

"Scared," Brendon said, sitting and crossing his legs. He held his hands in the air, making 'O's with his thumbs and index fingers, and again he shut his eyes.

"Yes," Megan said, also sitting. Gucci jumped onto her lap and she fluffed his fur. "I was scared. James is so mature, so grown up. He's got a big job, a future, he's kind and—"

"The opposite to Dylan." Georgie righted herself and sat like Brendon.

"Yes, that's exactly it."

"Dylan was always such a mummy's boy," Brendon said, tilting his chin. "I bet that's the last way you'd describe James."

Megan was quiet for a moment. Brendon was right. Dylan *was* a mummy's boy. James, on the other hand, was exactly the type of man she'd always hoped Dylan would become once he was a husband and a father. But she'd been a fool to get so far down the road with him that she'd stood in a white dress in a church. People didn't change because they had a ring on their finger or because they'd produced offspring. Dylan would be the way he was forever.

Thank goodness he was no longer part of her life.

"So you haven't seen him since last night?" Georgie said. "James, that is."

"No, I spotted my clothes spread over the floor." Megan groaned as she remembered hopping around naked, trying to untangle her underwear and get them on. She'd been able to hear James humming downstairs and her brain had felt foggy yet adrenaline had coursed through her veins. She'd just had to get out of there. Shrug off the night and escape into the day.

But now…

Now she didn't feel like that. She'd behaved badly towards James. What must he have thought when he'd found her gone? He'd been making breakfast for them, she was sure of it. She'd heard him banging around in the kitchen as she'd grabbed her purse and let herself out of the front door.

She'd only taken three steps at a walk then had burst into as fast a run as her red heels would take her. She dreaded to think what a sight she would have been to passers-by and to the taxi driver she'd hailed once on the main road. She'd hugged her arms around herself in the cab, the streets of London a blur as they'd moved through traffic. Her limbs had felt twitchy, her heart still pounding.

She'd just had to escape.

Get away.

But *why*?

"So," Brendon said, resting his arms down and studying Megan. "I think the best course of action now would be to call him and apologise."

"What?" Megan was horrified at the thought. "I can't do that, what the bloody hell would I say?" She paused. "And besides, I don't have his number."

"We can soon get that from the studio." Brendon waved his hand in a circle as though it was a minor detail.

"Yes, then you can call and say that you woke and remembered somewhere urgent you had to be," Georgie suggested.

"That's lame," Brendon said.

"And he knows I was only working at the office today." Megan sighed. "So that won't cut it."

"How about you woke in turmoil?" Brendon said. "He was so amazing, your night together was so utterly mind-blowing that your head and heart weren't functioning in unison. You had to get away, figure out your feelings and not be distracted by his incredible beauty and prowess between the sheets."

"Really?" Georgie said. "That's the best you can come up with?"

"Well, it's not that far-fetched." Brendon huffed. "I've had nights so good that the next day I've hardly been able to think straight. Moments, like flashbacks, keep attacking my mind. Little shivers run over my arms and tighten my belly. It's just memories, but still, enough to make my brain struggle to behave normally."

Megan thought about what Brendon had just said. She did indeed keep having delicious memories of her time with James. Everything about him had been so in tune with her. It was as if their pheromones matched—his scent, his taste, his touch—it had all been exactly what she'd needed.

She crossed her legs. They'd fitted so perfectly. It had been like a wonderful dance they hadn't needed to rehearse, both had instinctively known what the other wanted and needed.

She sighed and glanced at her mobile. Perhaps she should give him a ring. Figure out what to say, then call and apologise. If she were really lucky he'd maybe agree to meeting at Frank's for a drink sometime.

"So, who did you last have a night like that with, Brendon?" Georgie asked. "One that blew your mind."

"That would be telling." Brendon scooped up Gucci and hugged him close. He snuggled his face into Gucci's neck.

"So tell," Georgie said.

"That guy from Ritzy Rainbows."

"The one with shoulders the size of a tank?" Megan asked. She remembered Brendon going off with the huge bloke on a Friday evening a few months ago. She and Georgie had taken a cab home from Ritzy's soon after he'd disappeared into the darkness and they hadn't seen him all weekend. If she remembered rightly, Brendon had had a smile as wide as a Cheshire cat's all week and a lot of sexting had gone on between him and the mystery bloke for several days.

"Yes, that's the one," Brendon said, then frowned. "Shame he neglected to tell me he already had a boyfriend. A city bloke who was in Dubai on business."

"What a git," Georgie said.

"You never told us that bit." Megan's heartstrings tugged for Brendon. He got plenty of action but his heart was always left bruised.

"What was the point?" Brendon shrugged. "It was a few nights of fun, pretty damn hot fun, but that's all it was ever going to be. I'm lucky in the bedroom but unlucky in love."

"It won't always be that way." Megan pressed her hand over his. "There is someone out there who is perfect for you."

"Yes, you just have to keep looking," Georgie said. She held up her hand and the sunlight caught on her engagement ring. "Then you'll find the right man, like I have."

"I know." Brendon laughed. "But I'm having a great time looking. Trying them all on for size, so to speak."

Megan giggled and sat back on the sofa. Her friends always made her feel better even if they couldn't always come up with solutions to her problems or undo her mistakes.

"So did you make a start on my shoe design?" Georgie asked, also sitting on a soft chair and crossing her legs.

"Your bridal ones?"

"Of course." Georgie grinned. "What else?"

"Yes, I was thinking about ninety millimetres for the heel. That way you won't get any aches from being in them all day and dancing all night. Plus, even if you have a big veil or something, you'll still be shorter than Tom."

"That sounds fine. I couldn't walk in some of the super-high heels you wear."

"Sure you could. You just need to decide between ivory and cream satin then I'll get some samples for you to look at."

"Ha, go for cream satin, no way can our Georgie wear white."

"Hey." Georgie play-tapped Brendon around the head. "Watch it, or you won't be a bridesmaid."

Brendon's expression changed. "What?"

"Bridesmaid." Georgie shrugged. "Well who else did you think I was going to ask? I haven't got any sisters or female cousins. You two are my best friends, the ones I want to be there talking me down from Bridezilla moments in the run up to the big day." She looked between them. "So what do you think? Are you both up for it?"

A rush of excitement flooded Megan. This was good, this was moving on. Now they had Georgie and Tom's wedding to chat about, look forward to and plan. It would take her mind off the disasters that tailed her and give her a focus. "Of course," she said, flinging herself at Georgie. "Thank you for asking."

Georgie giggled and hugged her back.

Brendon joined in the group cuddle. "I want flowers," he said. "Not just a buttonhole but a proper bunch of flowers to hold. Trailing too, preferably gypsophila."

"You can have whatever you want," Georgie said, her eyes a little misty with emotion.

"Oh this is so exciting," Brendon said, clasping his hands beneath his chin. "Another wedding." He glanced at Megan. "Sorry, but you know, you didn't get married but the preparation was half the fun."

Megan smiled. "I guess so."

"We should go for drinks later to celebrate," Brendon said. "Champers, what do you think?"

Georgie glanced at her watch. "I can't. I have to go now. I'm meeting Tom at Marks and Spencer. We're doing a food shop."

"Oh, how utterly domesticated." Brendon tutted and rolled his eyes. "You're an old married couple already."

"And loving it." Georgie stood. "Here, open this, Megan." She tossed the white envelope at Megan.

Megan caught it and studied the printed letters. No surname or address, no stamp, just *Megan*. "Seems a bit odd."

"Probably a bill," Brendon said, smoothing his hand down Gucci's back and trying unsuccessfully to tame his wild fluff.

Megan poked her thumb into the corner of the envelope and prised it open. It contained a single sheet of white paper. She pulled it out.

Nothing.

It was totally blank.

"What does it say?" Georgie asked, craning her neck to look.

"It hasn't got any writing on it." Megan showed her. "How strange."

"Yeah, odd." Brendon scowled at it. "What's the point in sending someone a letter that doesn't have any writing on it?"

"And hand delivered," Georgie added.

"Perhaps it's a mistake. Maybe they put in the wrong sheet of paper."

They were silent for a minute. Megan had no idea what it was all about.

Her mobile trilled to life, breaking the quiet.

"Hello."

"Is that Megan Winter?" a woman asked.

"Yes, it is."

"This is Nancy Rider from *Ralph and Jayne*. We were thrilled with how your slot went on the show. We hope you were too?"

"Yes, absolutely." Megan did a thumbs-up sign to Brendon. "And that's great to hear. I really enjoyed presenting."

Brendon's eyes widened and he nodded.

"And what we'd really like to do," Nancy went on, "is offer you two more appearances talking about shoes for all seasons and occasions."

"More appearances." A flush of excitement went through her. "Really?"

"Yes, really. Ralph and Jayne thought you had great on-screen presence and will be very popular with viewers. You also ad-libbed with style, which is essential to live TV."

"Oh, well, thanks." She could feel her cheeks heating, her stomach clenching. This could be such a big break for her and Winter Shoes.

"So what do you say?" Nancy asked. "The first appearance would be tomorrow."

"Tomorrow?"

"Yes, I know it's short notice and you'd need to be at Grace Studios for nine in the morning then you'd be on at ten-forty-five. I can go through a standard contract and salary details when you get here."

"Wow, I mean, yes, that's sounds fine. Great." She was going to be on TV…again. *Ralph and Jayne really liked me.*

"Perfect, we'll see you in the morning. I'll leave a staff pass for you at reception so bring ID. Once you have that, head to Studio Four's hair and makeup. Will you be okay, it can be a bit of a rabbit warren?"

"I'll be fine. I managed last time."

"Good, have a nice evening then, Megan."

"You too." Megan ended the call.

"What in the sweet name of Jesus was that all about?" Brendon asked, standing and ramming his hands on his hips.

"Another appearance. They want me to go on Ralph and Jayne in the morning to do another shoe fashion presentation. Season shoes, occasion shoes, like bridal." She glanced at Georgie. "It's fabulous, an amazing opportunity and I think there will be one more after that."

"I told you they loved you," Brendon said, grinning manically. "Clearly they *really* loved you, and blimey, this could sky-rocket Winter Shoes into the stratosphere." He shook his head. "There is so much to do, so much to do. Come on, we should start planning. Where are those shoes that came in last week?"

"In the spare room." Megan's cheeks were aching from smiling so much. Her heart was trip-trapping along. Was she dreaming? She had to stop herself from pinching her arm to check she was awake.

Her phone rang again. "They must have forgotten to tell me something."

She glanced at the screen. Withheld number.

"Hello?"

No response.

"Hello, who's there?" she said. "I can't hear you."

Silence.

A chill dampened down her excitement of moments ago. Her scalp prickled and her stomach tensed. There was nothing wrong with the line…she could hear faint breathing. It was just someone listening to her, not replying.

Quickly she ended the call.

"Who was that?" Brendon asked.

"No one."

"No one?" Georgie repeated. "You don't look like it was no one. You've gone from being flushed to ghostly."

"Well it was someone," Megan said. "But I don't know who. I've had a few silent calls recently." She shrugged. "Kids messing about, probably. Got hold of my number and keep hitting redial."

"Mmm." Brendon reached for a file that held information on the next season's shoe order. "Odd letters and silent calls, just as well I'm moving in for the evening."

Megan couldn't deny that she was pleased Brendon was staying. The phone call and the letter had freaked her out a bit. Why would anyone use such passive, unproductive methods to get her attention? It just gave her the creeps.

Unless of course that was the intention—to creep her out.

14

The grip on her ankles dug to the bone, her toes were elongating, drifting into flames. Her heart beat so fast she feared for its survival and she couldn't catch her breath. All the time Dylan stared at her, his blue eyes penetrating to her soul like shards of ancient ice chipped from a glacier. The contrast of hot and cold, icicle and flame made her struggle all the more.

She had to get out of there.

She woke.

Her plush velvet curtains were the first thing she saw. The sunlight was pouring around them creating bright, skinny fingers over the wall. She sucked in a breath and willed herself not to leap from the bed—it wasn't a pit leading to Hell, it was just a mattress with Giovanna Valere bedding, nothing scary at all. Nothing that was going to gobble her up for all of time.

"Get a grip," she muttered. Her forehead was damp and the T-shirt she'd slept in clung to her breasts and back. "You've got a big day. No time for crazy dreams or paranoia."

She stood and walked to the bathroom. Her legs were a little weak as she climbed into the shower, her heart still beating rapidly.

Within a few minutes of standing beneath the warm water, though, she felt better. She had a lot to do. With Brendon's help the evening before, she now had her presentation all planned out. She was doing a feature on bridal shoes as that's where her mind had been focused of late. She had several designs to show off. She'd be fine, she knew her subject inside out, and Ralph, well, he was a pussycat, she was sure of it. Plus she'd felt confident in front of the camera. It was just one man after all, holding a piece of recording equipment. If she forgot about the several million viewers on the other side of the lens, it was easy-peasy.

She washed her hair with coconut scented shampoo and conditioner. Scrubbed with Molton Brown bodywash then wrapped herself in a thick towel. Brendon had suggested she wear fitted black cropped trousers with a low-cut cerise top, he'd said it was business-like yet sexy, sophisticated yet flirty. She was inclined to agree, it worked, especially with matching pumps. She slipped into her outfit and rubbed in her ridiculously expensive face cream. After a quick blast with the hairdryer she was set to go. She'd get camera-ready once at the studio.

"Damn!" She glanced at the clock. Time was ticking along. She grabbed the bags of shoes and the files of notes she needed, tucked her purse under her arm and dashed from the flat.

The sun was still shining and she breathed in the scent of freshly mown grass—the mower was being chugged around the small communal lawn by the gardener. It was a good day.

Or was it?

Like a lead weight landing in her belly she remembered the total mess that was her and James. What the hell was she going to do about it?

Nothing.

She didn't have time.

She hailed a cab and slid in, heavy bags and light jacket spreading on the seat as she flopped back against it.

"Grace Studios please."

"Yes, miss."

She crossed her legs and checked her fingernails—luckily the polish was unchipped. Would that weight in her belly lift over the course of the day? That feeling of having totally messed it up with a seriously hot guy who ticked every box she had ever wanted ticking?

She didn't have his number to call and apologise. She probably should ask at reception and get it. Now she was staff they might give it to her. She could call and say she'd had an urgent dentist appointment, or a meeting with her bank manager…or simply say she'd been spooked and had run.

It had all been too much too soon and she was still on the rebound from jilting Dylan.

Perhaps honesty was the best policy?

She tapped her toe in the air, stabbing towards the seat in front of her. No. She'd blown it. He'd think she was a silly little girl who'd created an illusion of sophistication yet beneath it all was messed up and only good at running.

She couldn't blame him for that.

The cab pulled up so she paid and jumped out, hauling her bags with her.

The studio stood imposing before her, stretching upwards to the blue sky. Last time she was here she hadn't noticed the massive scale of it, now she did and it dwarfed her.

"You can do this."

She walked to the entrance. A fountain sprinkled water from a contemporary chrome spout and it splashed on the black granite pavers before trickling in an 'S' shape to an ornamental drain.

Had James walked past this very fountain this morning? His feet treading where hers did now? Maybe he wasn't at the studio—he'd said their project was coming to an end. Perhaps he'd finished it and would be moving on to new things, preparing to expose more injustice in the world.

She slipped through the revolving door and her shoes tapped softly on the tiled floor.

The receptionist looked up as she approached. "Good morning."

"Hi. I'm supposed to collect a staff badge and head to Studio Four." Megan handed over her driving licence.

"Yes, of course." The receptionist smiled, revealing brilliant white teeth. She plucked a small clip-on laminated badge from a drawer. "Here you go. It doesn't have to be visible at all times but you should have it with you whenever you are in the building."

"Okay, thanks." Megan slipped the badge into her purse.

"Round to the left then follow the signs."

"Thanks. Have a nice day."

"You too."

Megan headed in the direction she'd gone in the day before. She had bags in each hand and her jacket looped over her arm. As she walked past the canteen she peered through the window. Was James in there?

Her gaze naturally landed on the table they'd sat at when sharing lunch—the one with the nice views over the studio garden. It was empty. The chairs at angles, as though someone had not long since left and hadn't bothered to push them in.

Suddenly the door was pushed open, and two men, talking loudly appeared before her.

One of them was James.

Her breath caught in her throat and her peripheral vision blurred slightly.

She'd been looking for him, yes, but she hadn't expected him to appear before her in such a burst of activity.

He glanced at her then back again, his eyes widening and his jaw slackening for a brief moment. Then his eyes narrowed and his mouth became a tight line.

The man with him held the canteen door open and looked at Megan. "Are you going in?" he asked with a smile.

"I…er…no." Megan considered him. He was tall and slim with blond hair slightly curled around his ears. He wore a checked red shirt over a white T-shirt and his jeans were ripped on the right knee.

"What are you doing here?" James asked, shoving his hands into his trouser pockets.

The hard tone of his voice served only to increase the weight in Megan's belly. She really had blown it with him.

He hated her.

She couldn't blame him.

"I've got more appearances on *Ralph and Jayne*. Fashion stuff, this season's must-haves, bridal, that kind of thing…" Her tongue felt tangled around the words. The skin on her brow prickled.

"You know each other?" the man with James said, letting the canteen door shut with a quiet whoosh.

Megan noticed that he had an American twang.

"Yes." James indicated Megan then his colleague. "Grant this is Megan. Megan, Grant, my co-director."

"Nice to meet you," Megan said, the tickly feeling on her brow travelling over her scalp and down her neck. She had to get out of there. She couldn't bear the irritated look on James' face. It was as if saying her name had left a bitter taste on his tongue.

"Ah…Megan…" Grant said, nodding slowly and a smile spreading on his face. "*The* Megan."

"What do you mean?" Megan asked.

"He doesn't mean anything." James threw a sharp-eyed glare at Grant. "Do you?"

"I guess not." The smile didn't drop from Grant's face.

It was clear to Megan that they'd talked about her. Her name was significant to Grant, which meant James must have told him about their date, their time together.

Oh God, had he told him about how she'd tumbled into bed with him?

Heat bloomed on her cheeks. Her belly tightened. She couldn't stand it.

Run.

Get out of there.

No. She couldn't keep running away from James. She'd wait until they left. Besides, her bags were too heavy.

"Well, I hope it goes well on the show," James said, stepping away.

"Yeah, live TV isn't easy. I admire you for it." Grant nodded and made no move to leave.

He had deep ocean-blue eyes and his lashes were sun-kissed. He also had a golden tan, one that looked as though it was well ingrained.

"Thanks," Megan said. "I'm no expert, but so far so good."

"And that Ralph..." Grant tutted and rolled his eyes. "Honestly, not that I have time to watch it, this one works my fingers to the bone, but from what I hear, he's a bit of a character."

"I can handle him." She glanced at James. He'd pulled his hands from his pockets and crossed his arms over his chest.

Megan looked at how his T-shirt stretched around his biceps. Only two nights ago she'd clung to those sculpted muscles. She'd been so consumed by him. Yet now he looked as if he'd happily switch to living on a different planet to get away from her.

"I bet you can," Grant said. "A gorgeous young thing like you. He'd be putty in your hands."

"Come on, Grant." James' voice was tight with tension. "These edits are not going to do themselves."

"See," Grant said, finally stepping away. "Slave driver."

Megan swallowed, her mouth suddenly dry. She looked at James but he'd turned and was striding down the corridor. His long paces making short work of the distance.

"Catch you around, Megan." Grant gave a playful wave then jogged after James.

She blew out a breath through pursed lips. Her heart was thudding and her knees jittery. But she hadn't run—she'd stood her ground even if it had been torturous. Even if it was clear she'd burned all her bridges with James, wrecked what had hardly even begun.

And it was all her own stupid fault.

She hoisted her bags onto her shoulder and headed for Studio Four. Now she knew that weight in her belly was there to stay. And she deserved it, to carry that ache, because for James to have behaved like that, when he was normally such a gentleman, she must have really upset him.

She found her way into hair and makeup and was greeted by Brendon, who'd made it into the studio before her.

"Hey, sweetpea, you're here." He gave her a brisk hug. "And looking fabulous in that outfit, perfect for a summer's day, don't you think Lisa?"

The woman to his left nodded. "Yes. Classic yet casual. I like it, a lot."

"Thanks." Megan rested her bags of shoes and files in the corner.

"Lisa is at your disposal," Brendon said. "And she's one of the best hair and makeup girls here, so use her well." He checked his watch. "You've got an hour and Nancy wants to run through the contract while you're getting ready. I'll let her know you're here."

"Thanks." Megan sat in a soft leather chair that faced a mirror.

Brendon disappeared out of the door, rushing in his usual frenetic manner.

Sometime later, Megan stared into the same mirror. The slot had gone well. The pictures she'd requested to flash on screen at various points in her presentation had appeared in order. Jayne had cooed lovingly over a pair of sparkling, sixty-millimetre heels that Megan had just supplied to her retailers—so she hoped they'd sell out pretty quickly—and she'd handled Ralph with ease.

Now that the excitement was over she suddenly remembered the strange note, the silent calls and the feeling of being watched. She shuddered and looked up into the corners of the makeup room. Were there cameras up there? Tiny hidden ones that were used for secretly watching guests and presenters get dressed ready for camera.

"Megan, for goodness' sake," she muttered. She was being paranoid. What the hell was the matter with her? Events were obviously playing with her nerves.

She re-applied her red lipstick then dropped it in her purse. It was time to go to the office and stop acting like a crazed woman. She had work to do, emails to check, plus her new assistant was starting in an hour and she needed to show her the ropes.

She packed up the shoes and secured the bags over her shoulders. Brendon had already left to work on another job and Lisa was on her break.

The corridor was empty and silent when she stepped out. As she walked along, to avoid thinking about her recent paranoia, she speculated about the things going on behind all the doors. Editing, more hair and makeup, meetings, celebrities working on projects. She wondered which one James was in.

She turned the corner towards the canteen.

Leaning against the wall, tapping on his iPhone, was James.

He had one knee bent, the sole of his shoe flat on the wall, and his head and shoulders stooped.

Megan hesitated. What should she do?

There was no one else around, no crowd to get swallowed up by. She had to say something. She couldn't just sneak past him.

He looked up. Saw her and swept his tongue out to lick his bottom lip.

"Hi…again…" she said.

"Good, you're here." He slipped his phone away and pushed away from the wall.

"You were waiting for me?"

"Yes." He sounded very sharp and determined.

"Why?"

"We need to talk." He reached for her hand and tugged her forward.

She followed for several paces, staring at his wide back. His shirt was a little creased, as though he'd been pressing against a chair for a few hours.

He opened a door and stepped inside, tugging her with him.

"What…?" she asked. "Where is this…?"

He shut the door.

Darkness engulfed them. She could hear him breathing. Her pulse was loud in her ears.

Suddenly a dim golden glow filled the room. The bare bulb above them spread weak light over a stack of cleaning products and mops.

"Megan," James said, stepping close.

She backed up. Her shoulders touched a shelf stacked with toilet rolls. He was so big, looming above her. His chest so wide and his face, his gorgeous handsome face, it seemed full of angst, the angles more defined than ever.

"What do you want?" she whispered, surrounded by the scent of his cologne.

"I would have thought that was fairly obvious."

She shook her head. "No."

"I want you." He cupped her jaw, his thumb resting over her cheek. "Don't you get that, Glitter?"

Oh God, he still wanted her? *Yes, he must do*. That flash in his eyes, desire laced with need. The touch of his hand, possessive yet gentle.

"But I…" She looked away. "I'm sorry."

"For disappearing on me…again?" he asked. "Or sorry you don't want me?"

"I am sorry for leaving yesterday morning. I don't know what got into me, it was all so fast."

"What was?" He lowered his head. "What was fast?"

His breath was fanned over her lips, his body heat radiating onto her chest.

"Us, it all happened so fast, and I'm still." She hesitated. "I'm just…"

"What?"

She was silent and glanced downwards.

"Tell me." He held her face with both hands and urged her to look up at him. "You're just what?"

She should tell him about jilting Dylan, she knew she should. About running out of a church packed full of their family and friends. But she couldn't. Shame ate away at her for letting the dysfunctional relationship go so far. Not to mention she knew that many people thought she was a total cow for what she'd done.

She didn't want James to think that of her. Of all the things he probably thought, she couldn't stand it if he thought she was a cow.

"Megan," he whispered, his mouth hovering over hers. "What is it?"

"I'm just stupid sometimes. I get freaked out. I don't know why." She looked into his eyes. "Can you forgive me?"

"I was so bloody angry with you yesterday," he said, slipping one hand around the back of her neck, then threading his fingers into her hair. “I thought I’d done something wrong. I couldn’t understand why you wouldn’t have told me if I’d messed up big time.”

“No, no, you did nothing wrong. It was all…perfect.” Oh and it had been, mind-blowingly, toe-curlingly perfect.

“Perfect,” he said, a slow smile stretching his lips. “I can live with that.”

Megan let her bags fall to the floor and slipped her hands around his waist, spreading her fingers wide and taking in the strong, tense muscles that lined his spine.

Right now she’d happily have his shirt vanish into thin air.

“I told myself not to want you,” he said, “that you’re only going to mess with my head, but the truth is…”

“What?” She drifted her hands up his back to his shoulders, pulled him closer.

“I just can’t help myself.” He kissed her.

Megan melted against him, pressing her body to his chest and gripping his hair.

Her heart rate rocketed. She wanted more, she couldn’t get close enough.

He groaned and darted his tongue into her mouth. “I can’t stop thinking about you,” he murmured, kissing her cheek. “Of having you in my bed.”

“Yes, me too.”

“Everything about you is so sweet.” He nibbled her earlobe. “The way you taste, how you respond to me…”

Arousal flooded Megan’s veins. She wanted all of that now. She pushed against him.

“Ah, yeah…” he muttered, scooping his other hand under her thigh.

Megan took the hint and wrapped her leg around his hip. "James." She gasped.

"I don't know when I last wanted someone so badly," he said, his voice a little breathless. "You're driving me crazy." He looked downward, watching his own movements as he stroked her through the thin top. "I want to strip you naked, touch you, make you scream my name."

"We can't, not in here." But damn, she was tempted. She glanced at the door, wondering if it had a lock.

"No?" He rubbed against her, through their clothes. "You sure?"

A thrill went through her. She needed him, in her bed, soon. It seemed he felt the same way. "Yes, I'm sure, not in here…but soon…somewhere else."

"When can I see you?" he asked.

"Tonight."

"It's too damn long to wait. I'm going to be in agony."

"You're a big boy." She grinned. "I'm sure you'll find a way to figure it out."

"I'm not so sure." He groaned.

She dropped her leg from around his hip and enjoyed a happy, fluttery feeling in her chest. He'd forgiven her. He wasn't mad anymore. And she'd make damn sure she made it up to him, big time. She kissed him again.

15

Megan looked at her phone. James Carter. That was the name next to the number ending in three twos. Two was her favourite number, so of course it made sense that was a connection to James.

They were meant to be.

It was all going to be all right.

And she could hardly wait until evening. A night of hot, sweaty fun was exactly what she needed, and what was even better, she knew James was up for the job. He could press all her buttons, make her gasp with delight and take her as high as a kite.

She squirmed a little on her office chair and watched as her new assistant, Enid, efficiently slotted files into the cabinet.

Nightfall couldn't come soon enough.

Georgie had come up trumps and after only a few hours Enid seemed very at home at Winter Shoes and was getting to grips with the straightforward way Megan had of doing things.

She had a greying bun that bobbed as she moved and wore a cream twinset complete with pearls. Megan was thrilled with the confidence she exuded and certainly her past experience was very impressive. Plus she seemed enthusiastic about the shoes and the marketing opportunities Brendon was working on.

All in all, she was perfect for the job.

The lone bridal shoe on a shelf by the window caught Megan's attention. She stared at the long, slim heel and the diamanté that caught the sunlight. Despite its pretty design, looking at it made Megan nauseous. It had become the symbol of her recurring nightmares.

It was time for it to go.

She stood and straightened her blouse—still a little creased from James' cupboard caress—and walked towards it. She had to stand on a stool to get it down and when she did, she thought how heavy it was. It was as if the sum total of what it represented—Dylan, running away, a future that would have dragged her under—had made the materials denser, thicker.

She held it at arm's length and walked to the bin, staring at the scraped heel where the gravel had chipped it. She pressed the pedal with her pink pump and the lid sprang upwards.

"Goodbye, forever," she muttered, dropping it in. She let the lid bang shut.

"Everything okay?" Enid asked, looking up from the new computer.

"Yes, fine, better than fine." Megan rubbed her hands together. "That shoe held bad memories and right now I haven't got room in my head for that kind of stuff."

"I totally agree, dear, out with the old and in with the new, that's what I always say."

Although the afternoon dragged for Megan—because she just wanted to be alone with James—there was lots to be getting on with. Things she'd had to put off because of dealing with more monotonous jobs. But with Enid firmly settled at her desk back at the office and fielding calls and emails, Megan was free to work on new designs and next week's Ralph and Jayne presentation.

As she let herself into her ground-floor apartment, her bones were weary yet her mind alive. Her future felt bright and full again. A wonderful contrast to only weeks ago.

She shut the door, dropped her keys on the side then picked up her mail. Two bills, a letter from a charity and something for the previous occupier who'd moved out years ago. And one white envelope with just *Megan* written on the front.

A wave of anxiety went through her. It was the same as the day before. No stamp, no address, clearly hand-delivered. And because her name was typed, it seemed the sender didn't want her to recognise their handwriting.

She walked into the kitchen and tore open the envelope.

Like before, the paper inside was blank.

She tutted, scrunched it into a ball then threw the letter into the bin. *What a waste of time.*

There was a sudden noise behind her.

Megan turned, pressing her hand to her chest to try to calm her thumping heart.

"I'm sorry, I didn't mean to startle you."

"Dylan, what the hell...?" Her stomach did a flip. It was the first time she'd seen him since she'd left him at the altar. He looked bigger than ever, wearing just a white vest top, his muscles pumped up. But his hair was a little wild, he was unshaven, which wasn't like him, and his eyes flashed the way they did in her dream.

"How did you…?" She glanced at the hallway. He didn't have a key, she knew he didn't. She'd made sure of that.

"You've always forgotten to lock the door when you walk in."

He was right, she did—he used to yell at her for it.

"You shouldn't be here." A tremble of nerves went through her. A menacing vibe was coming from him and his hands were curled into fists.

"Of course I should be here." He held out his hands and unfurled his fingers. "We need to talk. The way it ended…it was all wrong."

"We spoke on the phone the next day. Everything was said, there's nothing more to talk about." She put her hand in her jacket pocket and unlocked her iPhone, hoping Dylan wouldn't notice the movement. "You need to move on with your life. I am."

"How did I know you'd say that?" He rolled his eyes.

"Because it's the truth."

"No, it's not. I have no life now. You need to listen to me and believe me when I say I can make you happy. We are meant to be. Dylan and Megan Dunkin-Buckshaw, that's how it should be and it still can be. I need you to give me a second chance."

Megan shook her head and turned. She walked past the window to the fridge and opened the door. "Do you want a drink?"

"A Stella, if you have one."

How predictable.

As she reached into the fridge she pulled out her iPhone. She pretended to fuss for a moment getting a beer from packaging, yet she quickly texted Brendon.

Come quick. D here!!!!!

She hit send and plucked a bottle of Stella from the shelf, leaving the phone in the fridge to avoid risking Dylan seeing it when she removed her hand. "Here." She popped the lid, set the bottle on the island and glanced outside. It was getting dark, the cars on the road had their headlights on and glowed amber through the dusk.

She hoped Brendon wouldn't be long. He wasn't the toughest bloke, but right now it was the best she could do. Plus he was only a couple of minutes away, providing he was home, that was, and not still at the studio or out on a job.

James? Should she text James?

No. He didn't even know about Dylan and introducing her new boyfriend right now into this situation—with that manic look Dylan had in his eyes—it wouldn't go down well.

Besides, James only just thought she was the right side of sane as it was. Him finding out about Dylan would put him off forever. And that was the last thing she wanted.

Dylan walked from the doorway and farther into the room. She hoped he'd stay on the other side of the island but he didn't, he came around it and crowded her against the sink.

"Honeypie," he said, coming close. "I've missed you so much."

Megan gripped the counter behind her and pressed her bum against it, wishing she could make herself small, disappear even. That she could be anywhere but here.

Dylan ran the back of his index finger down her cheek.

"Don't," she said, as a quiver of distaste shot through her nerves. "And don't call me that."

"I've always called you that." He pushed a lock of hair behind her ear and smiled. "Because you're my honey." He moved his head closer. "And I've missed your sweetness."

She pressed her hand to his chest, hoping to prevent him coming nearer. "We're over. You have to understand that. There will be no second chance."

"No." He shook his head. "We're not over. This is just a little blip."

"It's one hell of a blip, Dylan. I left you in church, remember." Drastic measures were called for. No more pussyfooting around and worrying about his feelings. "I changed my mind. I decided I didn't want to marry you, remember? I left you at the altar."

"And you made me look a complete fucking fool in front of everyone. They were all talking about me. Feeling sorry for me, thinking I was a loser..." His nostrils flared and he slid his hand to the back of her head, balling her hair into his fist.

"Please, don't. Get off." She froze as her scalp complained at the sting, knowing movement would make it worse.

"Remember how good we were together," he said, speaking against her temple. "When I grabbed you like this." He wrapped his other arm around her waist and tugged her close. "And just took you. You used to love that, Megan. A bit of rough, a bit of fun." His breaths were loud. "You can't deny that."

"But it's over now." She pushed him, throwing a good dose of effort into shoving at his chest. It was true she had loved him once, or thought she had, but it was over.

He released her and stepped back, a smile on his face. "Oh yeah, you remember everything, and you miss it too. I can tell. Look at you, flushed, breathing fast. It was always the same, whenever we were near each other clothes had to come off." He reached for the base of his T-shirt. "Like now."

"No, seriously. We can talk if you want but not…"

He cocked his head and chuckled but thankfully left his T-shirt on. "It will remind you of what you threw away. Of what you can have again, right now."

"I know what I threw away, Dylan. And I threw it away because I didn't want it." She paused. She'd thought she had wanted it once, but no, she hadn't…it had all crashed down around her. The truth had flared in her face. "I didn't want *you*, Dylan. I'm sorry, but I didn't and I still don't want you."

He jerked his head, as though he'd been slapped across the cheek.

A stab of regret went through Megan. If only it could have been different. If only no one needed to get hurt. She wasn't proud of causing the pain in his eyes.

He thrust his hand through his hair and looked at the floor. "I know I wasn't perfect, but I tried, for you."

"I know you did."

The anger seemed to have left him, as had the confidence. Now it was all about sadness, sorrow.

"I just need you to give me a chance, Megan. Another go. I'll fix it, I promise."

"No. I can't do that." She swallowed. "I'm getting on with my life, my career, it's feeling good." She was going to add that it felt good to be herself, without worrying about him and his swinging moods and beer drinking.

A low groan left his chest and he squeezed the bridge of his nose.

For the first time ever, Megan saw a tear slide down Dylan's face.

"I'm so sorry," she said, closing the gap between them and resting her hand on his shoulder. God, could she feel more awful? "Really I am. But I can't conjure emotions that aren't there anymore."

"But they were. Love *was* there."

"A long time ago. At the beginning. But I'm not ready to get married. I should have realised that sooner." She stroked his shoulder. "And I apologise profusely for that."

"That's okay. I accept your apology." He looked up, hopeful, and dashed the rogue tear away. "And look, I had this done, for you." He gripped the base of his vest and tugged it off.

He dropped the vest to the floor and patted his hand over the gaudy red rose that was inked over his right pectoral. "A rose, your middle name, red for love, over my heart. Now you'll always be with me, part of me. Nothing can change that."

Megan stared at the tattoo. She'd hoped the rumour had been false, but now, seeing the ugly design on his skin made her stomach lurch. She was just glad he hadn't had *Megan* scrawled through it. "It's…nice."

"It's more than nice, it's a symbol of our love. Our endless love."

What was the matter with him? He'd always been stubborn but this was really taking the biscuit. It was as if he'd become deaf to anything he didn't want to hear. "Dylan, I understand that you still have feelings for me."

"Love you."

"Love me even, but I don't love you, not anymore."

"But you used to love me, you said it lots of times. And you can again, I know it." He shot out his hands and pulled her near. "I love you so much."

"Dylan!"

His lips pressed down on hers. Hard and unmoving, and his hands roamed her body squeezing her close, clamping her to him.

Megan kept her mouth shut tight. "Mmmpfh…"

He pulled her nearer and his tongue penetrated her lips.

Anger rose within Megan. Indignation that Dylan thought he could get her affection like this. She drew her foot back and kicked him as hard as she could in the shin.

He snapped backwards, releasing her. "Ow, what the…!" He bent his knee and clutched his lower leg. Hopped on the spot.

"Seriously!" she said, wiping her mouth with the back of her hand. "What part of *I don't want you* don't you get, you moron?"

"What the hell is going on?" Brendon rushed into the room, arms in the air and a yellow and black scarf flapping about his neck. Gucci barked around his ankles excitedly, making figures of eight when Brendon drew to a halt.

Dylan spun around with a glowering look on his face. "What the hell are you doing here?"

Megan breathed a sigh of relief. *Thank goodness.*

"Dylan, long time no see," Brendon said, stooping to retrieve Gucci. He was breathing hard.

Gucci spotted Dylan and his lips curled back as he let out a long, low growl. His small sharp teeth flashed and his hackles rose.

"I bloody hate that dog," Dylan shouted, standing on both legs again and pointing at Gucci. "Keep it away from me."

"Yes, well, he's not too fond of you. I guess you could say he's a good judge of character." Brendon clenched his jaw. "Behave and I'll keep him under control."

Gucci barked again, as if trumpeting his fierceness.

Brendon ruffled his hair then straightened his sparkly blue collar.

"Don't tell me what to do," Dylan said, walking to the island and reaching for his Stella. He took a long slug. His gulps were noisy and his head tipped back.

Brendon widened his eyes at Megan. "What's going on?" he mouthed.

Megan shook her head and glanced out of the window. A sleek black car pulled into the passing traffic. It's headlights on full beam and its engine roaring.

"So," Dylan said, turning to face Brendon. "What are you doing here?"

"I'm here to see my friend." Brendon nodded at Megan. "But more to the point, why are you here?"

"I'm here to see Megan obviously. My fiancée."

"Ex-fiancée." Megan added. "We're over, finished, remember." A flashback besieged her. Running down the aisle. Dream mixed with reality. A sudden urge to run overtook her. She glanced at the door.

"I don't think you're thinking straight, honeypie," Dylan said, his voice mellowing again. "I have so much to offer you. We have a bright future." He paused, a smile stretched his mouth but didn't quite reach his eyes. "And we'd make beautiful babies."

"Oh my God, you are living in cloud cuckoo land," Brendon scoffed. "You're not going to be making any babies with our Megan. She doesn't want your babies. Why don't you get that? She's so over your DNA now and she's all about finding someone new."

"What the bloody hell has all this got to do with you?" Dylan scowled and rounded his shoulders. His arms hung at his sides, ape-like, and he took a step closer towards Brendon.

A rush of panic flooded Megan. That was Dylan's attack mode. She recognised it well from his drunken nights out when he'd decided to get aggressive at the end of the evening. Except this was way more dangerous—because from what she could tell he wasn't drunk and his thick-muscled aim was likely to land on target.

Brendon's nose *the* likely target.

But Brendon didn't seem worried. He placed a hand on his hip and stared at Dylan. He was only a fraction of the weight Dylan carried but he looked puffed up and ready to fight.

She'd never loved her friend more than in that moment.

"I'll tell you what it is to me," Brendon said. "Megan is a special woman who deserves more than a mummy's boy, a drunken slob and an oaf who only thinks of himself. I care about her as if she were my own sister—"

"Ha, ha, sister, that's right." Dylan clapped and pointed at Brendon's groin. "Because I don't have to worry about you ever wanting to get off with her."

"Dylan," Megan said. "What's got into you?"

"Him." Dylan continued to shake his finger in Brendon's direction. "Why is he here? We need space, privacy to work this out."

"There is nothing to work out."

"We were just getting started." He waggled his eyebrows.

"No we weren't. I think you should leave." Megan rubbed her hand over her forehead. If only he would just go. Go and leave her alone.

"You heard her," Brendon said. He jabbed his thumb over his shoulder. "Time to sling your hook. Go, be off with you."

"No, you fuck off." Dylan took a step closer to Brendon. "Yeah, you go, right now."

Gucci went into a frenzy of barking. He managed to growl at the same time and he writhed in Brendon's arms as if desperate to be free and snap at Dylan.

"Keep that dumb mutt under control." Dylan came to a halt and eyed Gucci warily.

"I will if you leave within the next ten seconds, then he's loose." As if to prove the point, Brendon held Gucci forward.

The nipping jaw frenzy increased, as did Gucci's scrabbling to be free.

Dylan turned to Megan.

For a moment she saw a flash of vulnerability in his eyes. He was at his wits' end, scraping the barrel for reasons why she should go back to him, give him another chance. He'd never particularly got on with Brendon, or Georgie for that matter, but he'd never actually been rude to them. Not like this.

"Dylan," she said. "There really is nothing left for us."

"Don't say that. There has to be." He walked up to her and took her hands in his.

She resisted then pulled away, clutching her hands to her chest and retreating. Dylan didn't deserve her hate, but he did have her pity.

Pity that she'd led him so far down the road that had their future stamped all over it.

She'd walked away feeling refreshed, new, excited about what life had in store. Yet it was clear she'd devastated him, wrecked his life and his soul.

Next time, if there was a next time mapped out in the Heavens for her, she'd have to be much more careful. Play the game better, handle hearts with more consideration. Treat hopes and dreams like the delicate webs of glitter they were.

"I have this." Dylan dug into the pocket of his sweats, his fingers scrabbling at the base. "For you."

"What?" Megan said, shifting from one foot to the other. She wanted to be kind, she really did, but she couldn't take much more. She thought of James and how he would never behave the way Dylan was, she was sure of it. Even when she'd seen him outside the canteen with Grant and he'd clearly been upset about their situation, he'd still maintained calm control. He exuded gentlemanly politeness. Oh, except when they were in a cleaning cupboard and hadn't been able to keep their hands off each other—that hadn't been so polite, the way he'd kissed her and whispered in her ear exactly what he wanted to do with her.

A shiver of excitement spread through her. James would be here soon. She just needed to get rid of Dylan…fast. She'd moved on, well and truly. She'd had a bite of something much more to her taste and there was no going back.

"Here." Dylan stepped up to her, arm outstretched. In between his thumb and index finger was a silver ring with a large ruby set in it.

"What's that?" Megan asked.

"It's a new beginning, a new us." Dylan dropped to one knee and looked up at her, his eyes pleading.

"Let's start fresh, wear this new ring, one that signifies rising from the ashes."

"Oh my giddy heart, he's only getting poetic!" Brendon paced to the window and flung one arm in the air. "Praise the Lord, Dylan, you old romantic." He turned. "But it's too little too late."

Dylan ignored Brendon. His gaze didn't leave Megan's. "I mean it. We can be a phoenix together. It all collapsed around us, and I take part of the blame for that. I know I have to. But please, let's show the world how strong we are. How unbeatable we are. Let's climb out of the pit we fell into and rise stronger than ever." He held the ring closer to Megan. "Marry me. Not tomorrow, not next week, but at some point in our lives. This ring signifies a commitment and a promise, it doesn't have to be anything more than that, honeypie."

"I can't marry you." Megan was aghast. He really was delusional.

"Not now, we have to rebuild. But in the future we can marry." He took hold of her left wrist and poised the ring over her finger.

"No." She snapped her hand free. "No, this is crazy, *you're* crazy." Had she ever really known this man? How could he be so mistaken in her feelings for him that he thought she'd marry him—again? "You have to leave, Dylan. Now."

"No."

"Yes." She folded her arms and gestured towards the door. "Leave this minute or I'm calling the police."

"On it." Brendon held up his iPhone. "What was the number again…? Oh yes, nine, nine, nine."

Dylan made a noise not unlike a growl and stood. He slipped the ring back into his pocket. "You're making a mistake. Both of you." He swung his glare from Megan to Brendon then back to Megan. "I'm the best thing that ever happened to you. Without me you wouldn't have been brave enough to set up your business, you wouldn't be on bloody TV, you wouldn't be able to afford any of this." He swung his arm around, indicating her apartment.

"I've achieved all of this on my own." Megan shoved her hands on her hips. "And I've still got lots more I want to achieve." She nodded at the door. "Now go, before the police get here and I'll tell them it was all a mistake. If you're still here when they arrive I'll tell them you tried to force yourself on me, which you did."

His top lip curled into a snarl then he reached for his vest and balled it into his fist. He turned and loped from the room, head down and shoulders swinging. Within a few seconds, the sound of the front door slamming echoed.

16

James
Seven hours earlier

James opened the door to the Studio Three corridor and stuck his head out. All was still and quiet. He felt like a naughty schoolboy hiding in a broom cupboard as he was. But equally he couldn't remember when he'd last felt so good. Being with Megan gave him that euphoric feeling. It seemed she'd got under his skin, into his mind and was wheedling her way into his heart.

"All clear," he said tugging her out by the hand. He pulled her close and set a quick kiss on her lips. He just couldn't help himself, he wasn't ready to say goodbye yet, even though he had to. And he certainly wasn't ready to release her from his embrace. Having her near felt so right, so perfect.

She pulled back after a moment. "I'll see you later then." She stroked her hand down his arm, shoulder to elbow, smoothing his short-sleeved shirt.

The heat of her palm, just through clothing, sent tingles over his flesh. "Yes, you have my number now. Call me if something comes up, or if you're free sooner. If not I'll come over this evening after work. I'm not sure what time it will be, though."

"That's okay." She smiled. "Though I can hardly wait."

He loved the way her eyes sparkled. She wanted him the way he wanted her. Seeing the reflection of desire just made him ache all the more to be alone with her. How had he got so lucky? He'd forgotten how sweet it was to have a woman in his life. And he wanted more—he wanted more of Megan Rose Winter. She was the woman in his life now. She'd been on the periphery, the outskirts, admired from afar, but now… Now she was slap bang in the middle and he wanted it to stay that way.

"We can go out for dinner," he said, suddenly panicking that she'd think he was only coming over for sex. Which he kind of was, but it wasn't just that, he needed to be with her—that was his most basic need. Just to be in her presence.

"Or I could cook for us." She swept her tongue over her bottom lip. "Maybe it would suit us better to stay in."

"I like the way you think." He grinned. "I'll bring wine."

"White, I'll do chicken." She paused. "If that's okay with you? Do you like chicken?"

"Love it." If she'd said she was cooking crow, he would have agreed to it.

"Okay, see you later." She gathered her bags, positioning the straps on her shoulders and hoisting them upwards.

"Do you want a hand with them?" They looked heavy. He worried about her slender limbs carrying all that weight. It couldn't be good for her.

"I'm okay. I'm stronger than I look." She flashed him a cocky grin then turned.

He leant back on the wall, the way he had been when waiting for her, and watched her walk down the corridor away from him. She had such a sassy roll to her hips and her hair hung low, swinging left to right with each pace.

She turned the corner towards reception, and he let out a sigh. It was time to go back to Grant and finish the editing. They were on the final, final stages and he hoped to get it wrapped up and delivered to the board by the end of the day, tomorrow lunchtime at the latest.

All the more reason to celebrate with Megan tonight. It had been a long, gruelling project.

His phone vibrated in his pocket and he tugged it out. The screen flashed up with the name Rue Skimmer – his boss back in LA.

"Hey, Rue, how are things?"

"James, good to catch you, never know what damn time it is over there."

"It's midday. You must be up early."

"Yeah, Diane's got me on some crazy-assed health kick which means a power smoothie at the crack of dawn. Hopefully it won't last long but I've learnt it's easier to go along with it and let these fads run their course than try to resist."

"Sounds fun."

"It's not. But it does mean I can make a few calls." He paused. "How's it going over there in London? *Poor Choices* nearly wrapped?"

"Yep, should have it to you within hours."

"You pleased with it?"

"Yes, it's got to the heart of the matter for sure. Some powerful interviews and images."

"Great, that's why we pay you."

James thought he heard him drinking. No doubt his power smoothie.

"And so," Rue went on, "you and Grant are coming straight back to LA, right?"

"Well..." Thoughts of Megan went through James' mind. If he hadn't met her he'd likely be on the first plane out of London, needing sun, sea and the LA vibe, but now...now things were different. He wanted, no, needed to be with her. Wherever in the world Megan Rose was, was where he wanted to be, for now at least.

"Good, book on the first plane back. I need you to stand in for Leon Walder as of Monday, he's gone AWOL."

"Leon Walder?" James rubbed his forehead. Leon Walder directed low-brow documentaries and used Hollywood stars and starlets to present them. The last one being about boob-job botches and featuring ditzy blonde one-hit wonder, Daisy Gardner. James had watched it, but only because it had been on when he'd been catching up on some paperwork and he'd wanted to know what all the fuss was about Leon's series—he still didn't know.

"What do you mean AWOL?" James asked, taking a few paces across the corridor.

"Well, it's no big secret he's a fan of the sauce. Seems he checked into rehab for the weekend—who the hell gets rehabilitated in a weekend, for Christ's sake?—but he disappeared in the middle of the night. Gone, vanished. They just couldn't find him in the morning."

"What? Really?" James didn't like the bloke much but still, anything could have happened. "Is he okay, though?"

"Yeah, he'll turn up. He was spotted on CCTV leaving a Palm Springs bar with two bimbos, all propping each other up. Likely he'll be found by some poor cleaner in a motel, and he'll be wondering what the hell happened to the last week and then he'll find himself back in rehab."

James sighed. "Which means there's no one to direct his latest…documentary." James struggled to even call it a documentary. It certainly wasn't his sort of documentary.

"Exactly. Which is where you come in. We've got Tate Simmons presenting. He's massively popular right now and in great demand. He's starting on a movie in a few weeks so there's no time to lose. I need you and Grant back here."

"And what's it about?" James screwed up his eyes. He hardly dared ask. "Walder's latest project, that is."

"It's a fly on the wall about a real life Baywatch team at Santa Monica Beach."

James couldn't hold in a groan. "Really."

"Oh come on. I know it's not going to win you a globe or a gong but people are interested in this shit."

"Shit, that's exactly right."

His boss tutted. "I'm sorry it's not political enough for you—"

"Or relevant to the majority of society."

"But you're the only one and…" He paused. "We do pay your damn wages."

"Yeah, yeah, I know." And very handsome wages they were too. "I'll do it, but when I present to the board next month, for my next personal project, I'll hope this favour will be taken into account."

"You have my word." Again Rue slurped on his drink. "And, James, try to be nice to Tate. It's not his fault he's a pretty face but not much else."

"Yeah, I'll try." James ended the call and shoved his phone away. It seemed his time with Megan was going to be cut short after all.

Suddenly his celebratory mood waned. If only he had another month on *Poor Choices*.

James weaved through the London traffic towards the area of town Megan lived. He'd showered and dressed quickly, applied cologne and brushed his hair, all the time warring with the pleasure the evening would hold and the sadness that it was likely the last time they'd get to see each other for a while.

Maybe he could come back to London before his next project. Take some downtime, and spend it wining and dining Megan, taking her to the cinema, the theatre, for walks in the park. Yes, that's what he would do.

He stopped at a red light and tapped his fingers on the steering wheel. Why the hell did LA and London have to be so damn far apart? And why had bloody Walder gone on a bender and screwed up not just his own life, but James' too?

The driver in the car behind him honked his horn. The traffic lights had changed. James raised his hand in apology and carried on down the high street. It was getting dark, he'd left later than he'd planned but all was good. They'd finished the editing by staying an extra hour and now he had nowhere to be in the morning.

Thoughts of waking up with Megan made him smile. She'd be there. Where could she run to when they were at her place? He'd get to finally have breakfast with her, see her hair mussed from their night-time activities, perhaps even get to give her a soap down in the shower. Damn, that was a nice thought, seeing and feeling Megan when she was all wet, warm and sudsy…

He shifted on the seat. He really had to get a grip of his testosterone. It was raging.

A sudden thought entered his mind.

What if Megan came with him to LA?

Sure it was moving things quickly, but hey, who had time to hang about in life? He wanted her and was pretty sure she wanted him too.

She could come for a holiday, an extended holiday if she wanted. He'd only be at work in the day, they'd have long sunny evenings together. He could take her to the swankiest eateries, for walks on the beach, perhaps they could take a trip to Vegas and throw some dice.

Excitement tickled over his skin and he pulled in a deep breath. Maybe things would go further and she'd set up a branch of Winter Shoes out there, on Rodeo Drive. *Wow, that'd be amazing, she'd love it.* He'd back her if she needed it, though she seemed to be managing pretty well on her own—she was an independent, successful woman who knew what she wanted and went after it.

Well, sometimes she ran from it first.

He smiled a little indulgently, knowing that he'd caught her in the end.

Yes, that's what he'd do. They'd eat dinner, drink champagne, he'd kiss her all over, then he'd ask her to come out to his place in LA. With a bit of luck she wouldn't be able to resist, and he'd spoil her rotten—she didn't have to doubt that for a second.

The low-rise apartment where Megan lived came into view. He was lucky and found a spot just fifty yards from the path leading to her home and right beneath a street lamp. He drew to a halt and killed his lights, turned off the engine. He grabbed the chilled bottle of Moët he'd picked up from his local off-licence and got out of the car.

His stomach was tense, though he was looking forward to their evening. Seeing her smile, hearing her voice, kissing her lips—it was all so good. On top of that he had quite a proposition to put on the table.

He dodged a jogger wearing a flashing headlight strapped to his brow, then strode to apartment six. He started to rehearse in his mind what he'd say. How he'd ask her. Should he show her a picture of his Malibu pad? The views of the Pacific and down towards Santa Monica were stunning—surely that would sell it to her if she had any doubts.

Doubts. Damn it. In his fantasy her face lit up at the suggestion of coming to the States with him. In his fantasy she threw her arms around him telling him what a perfect idea it was and when were they going?

He hoped to hell the reality matched that fantasy. She'd love LA, it would match her sparkly personality, her glittery shoes, her love of glamour.

All she had to do was say yes.

As he walked to the main entrance, he saw movement in Megan's kitchen window. It was her.

His heart flipped.

His steps faltered.

The window was brightly lit, no curtains or blind drawn, and from the darkness it seemed the room was like a TV screen.

She had company.

He stopped.

She had *male* company.

A sinking feeling landed like an anchor in his belly. He couldn't see Megan's face. Her back was to the window, her hair catching the light from the overhead spots in the kitchen. But the beefy guy she was with clearly knew her well.

It was the expression on his face that told the story. It was full of adoration and longing and he had a softness in his eyes as he looked at her.

This unknown man, who James hated on sight, walked up to Megan and seemingly caressed her cheek.

She didn't move.

James increased his grip on the neck of the bottle of Moët.

What the hell is going on?

The guy pushed a lock of Megan's silky hair behind her ear. A smile spread on his face as he spoke, his head lowering to her lips.

James thought he might puke. His stomach churned. Everything he'd thought he had to look forward to, not just for the evening ahead, but for the weeks ahead, beyond, slipped like sand through a timer. Falling from his grasp.

He sucked in a breath, it was like breathing in treacle.

The scene before him unfolded as if he were watching a horror movie in slow motion. The man with Megan dipped his head so low James wasn't sure if he was kissing her. He must have been because he slid his fingers through her hair, bunching it at her nape, the way lovers do. He then spoke against her temple.

The hairs on the back of James' neck bristled. What the hell was he saying? If it was how much he adored her, what he wanted to do with her, then damn him, they were James' words to say to Megan, not this…imposter's.

But maybe he wasn't.

Perhaps James was the imposter and this was the man in Megan's life. Could he have got it all wrong? Had Megan ran, twice, because she was two-timing a steady blond boyfriend that she was keeping a secret from him? It was possible, she was beyond gorgeous, stood to reason she'd have more than one suitor on her radar. But why would she lie?

He continued to watch Megan through the window. He knew he shouldn't, he should turn and leave and not torture himself with watching her and this man for another moment.

Had she forgotten about their evening arrangement? Had he said a later time? Confusion buzzed through him like a swarm of bees. His mind felt fudged and his temper simmered towards boiling point.

But he had no claim on her. They'd only been on one official date, enjoyed a night of fun, yes, but still, he had no right to storm into her apartment and demand to know who the hell this man was.

Much as he wanted to.

It was like he'd said to her before. He wasn't in the habit of being with women who didn't want to be with him.

He heard footsteps in the distance, someone running. The flashing jogger on his way home probably. James glanced left and right, checking it wasn't some crazed person. He spotted a man heading his way, scarf flying behind him and a little brown dog galloping at his feet.

He turned his attention back to the window. Megan was still facing into the room. The guy gripped his T-shirt and pulled it over his head, revealing gym-buffed muscles, likely steroid enhanced. He tossed the material aside.

"Oh, God," James muttered. Was he really going to witness this? Surely they'd shut the damn curtains.

The couple connected—him pulling Megan close with his thick arms and kissing her passionately.

James turned. Pain shot through his chest and his head thumped with an impending migraine.

"Excuse me, excuse me, emergency, emergency, I..."

James stepped aside as the tall, thin guy who'd been running with the dog at his feet dashed up the path.

"Oh...it's..." the man said, slowing for a brief second and staring at James. Recognition flashed over his eyes.

"Sorry, go ahead." James held up the redundant bottle of bubbly and let the man past.

He was clearly in a wild hurry. Unlike James, who now had an empty evening ahead of him. Maybe he would just get straight on to the airlines and book a flight home. The sooner the better.

He stomped back down the path and to his car. He was angry, sad, furious and disappointed.

Women!

He never quite got it right. Either there wasn't enough time for dating and fun times or there was but not the right woman. He'd really thought Megan might be the one.

For crying out loud, only minutes ago he'd been imagining her on his balcony, in a bikini, sipping cocktails, enjoying dips in the ocean, smiling at him in that sexy way she did when he came in the front door.

He'd thought she'd wake stretched out in his bed, the sounds and scents of the waves filtering through the room and invading her dreams. He'd be there next to her, holding her as she came around.

Industry functions were usually lonely affairs for James. He never took a date, preferred the company of colleagues. But that would have all changed if Megan had come to LA with him. He'd have been proud to have her on his arm—she'd have put all the others to shame no matter how beautiful they'd thought they were. She'd have shone like the brightest star on the red carpet. Everyone would have been envious that she was his. The press would have been falling over themselves to take her picture and she'd have graced glossy magazines with her fresh beauty and seductive smile.

He clicked his key fob and his car beeped to life. He tossed the bottle into the back and dropped onto the driver's seat.

Pipe dreams. That's all that had been. Having Megan in LA wasn't going to happen. She was perfectly at home in London with her secret man and was right now showing him all her moves.

Another wave of nausea attacked James. He pressed his lips together and started the engine. It should have been him in there with her. Holding her, kissing her.

It should be me!

He indicated and checked his mirror. The traffic had eased a little and he pulled out on the main road, revved the engine and whacked up a gear.

A car behind beeped, one he hadn't realised was quite so close—his mind was clearly elsewhere. He tightened his grip and pushed his foot to the floor. Banged up another gear and let the roar from the exhaust fuel his frustration.

The sooner he was out of London the better.

17

Megan

Brendon looked at Megan and shook his head. His eyes were wide and his face pale. "Fuck a duck," he said, before setting Gucci on the floor then rushing to the hallway.

Gucci followed, yapping insanely.

"I'm gonna make sure this door is well and truly locked once and for all," Brendon shouted.

The deadbolt clicked then the chain rattled. Megan blew out a long, low breath. Her knees felt weak and muscle knots had formed around her shoulder blades.

"We don't want any more raving loonies wandering in here." Brendon appeared again. He stood in the doorway and tugged his scarf from around his neck. He threw it with a flourish onto the sofa. "I guess that's how he got in. He just wandered through the unlocked door as if he lived here." He scowled at Megan.

Her eyes stung, tears were threatening, and her throat felt thick. She was awash with emotions, but right now, feeling stupid for having got into that situation with Dylan was the overwhelming one. It didn't help that Brendon was now looking at her like she was up for a gold medal in the idiot Olympics. "Yes."

He tapped his hair, checking it hadn't shifted from his trademark flick. "Georgie only told you about that yesterday."

"I know. And it won't happen again. Not now." Her voice quivered on the last word. She turned, went to the kitchen window and quickly drew the blind. The thought that Dylan might still be out there, looking in made her feel violated, intruded upon. She didn't want Dylan in her life ever again.

If she'd ever been in any doubt about that, the last ten minutes had laid it to rest.

"Hey, you okay?"

She felt Brendon's hand on her shoulder. His softly spoken words and presence released the sob that had collected in her chest. It bubbled up, a big well of air that burst from her mouth and vibrated through her ribs.

"Hey, hey, it's okay, you're okay now."

He pulled her close, setting her face against his neck and circling her body. He rubbed his palms up and down her back and over her shoulders. "He's gone. It's okay, there, there…"

Megan screwed up her eyes but tears still escaped. She'd never meant to wreck a man. Never meant to make him a danger to her. But it had certainly felt like that when he'd grabbed her, kissed her. She was no match to his strength and if Brendon hadn't turned up when he had—it didn't bear thinking about.

"Shh…" Brendon said against her head. He stroked her hair, over and over. "Shh…shh…"

But she couldn't. The tears kept coming, as did the shakes. She gripped his sweater and locked her knees to prevent them from buckling. It was all such a mess.

God, imagine if I'd had to get the police here? Imagine if Brendon couldn't persuade him to leave. And Gucci…

"Is Gucci…okay?" she asked, pulling back and looking for the little dog that had defended her so valiantly. "Where is he?"

"He's fine. Perfectly fine." Brendon manoeuvred her so she could see the opposite end of the room. "Look."

Gucci was indeed fine and happily humping Megan's cat doorstop. His little body was infused with even more enthusiasm than usual.

"He was so brave." Megan sniffed.

Brendon released her and reached for the kitchen roll. "He's never liked Dylan. Remember that time when he chewed his new Nikes?"

"God, yes, he went ape. And that time…" Megan paused to gulp in air. Her sobs were under control but her chest was still heaving. "When he peed on him, just before…he went to that job interview."

"Bloody hell. I'd forgotten about that. Dylan went so red I thought he was going to blow a gasket. Steam came out of his ears."

Megan laughed, a little hysterically. She dabbed at her wet cheeks with the tissue and licked her dry lips. "Thank you for coming round so quickly."

"Thank goodness I did." Brendon wiped the back of his hand over his forehead. "Had to run like the wind, mind you."

"I'm glad you're fit."

He laughed at that. "I think it was fuelled by adrenaline. When I saw your text, the brevity of it sent alarm bells off in my head. I knew whatever was going down wasn't good."

"It wasn't."

"And man alive, that tattoo." He took Megan's hand and steered her to the sofa. "Sit."

She sat, glad to take the weight off her legs. "I know, not the most stylish bit of artwork."

Brendon pulled the main curtains in the living area then went back to the kitchen. "I trust you have wine, we need some, medicinal purposes of course."

"Yes, there's red open." She laced her fingers together and hoped the shaking would stop soon. "Make mine large."

"Already done that." He walked over and set two full-to-the-brim goblets on the table before her. "Because I think you're going to need it."

"I do need it."

"But there's something else."

The slow, serious way Brendon spoke sent a chill over Megan's skin. He had a slight frown marring his usually smooth brow and his lips were pressed tight together.

"What? What is it?"

"Take a sip."

"Tell me."

"Sip."

She did as he'd asked, letting the rich berry flavour spread on her tongue.

"There, so tell me."

"When I was running, up the path, coming here…"

"Yes." She made a circle with her hand. "What?"

"I saw someone." He shook his head. "Or at least I think I saw someone, I couldn't be one hundred per cent sure, but I think…"

"Who?" Megan clamped her hand over her chest. "You're worrying me, Brendon. Who did you see and why can't you be sure?"

"Well I've never seen him in real life, have I?"

"You're talking in riddles." Irritation swarmed over her.

"I've only Googled him, not had the pleasure…" He paused. "Were you expecting company tonight?"

The room began to spin, her ears buzzed.

No. It couldn't be true.

"Tell me who you saw, Brendon, or I swear I'll…"

"What? You'll what?"

"I'll…I'll…" She couldn't think straight—it was as if all the neurons in her head had disconnected.

"Hot Guy. I saw Hot Guy, standing out there, on the path." Brendon pointed at the kitchen window.

"James," Megan whispered. "James was here?"

"Well no, not here, out there. Standing on the path, looking in."

"No." She shook her head. "Why would he do that? Why wouldn't he come in?" She stared at the blinds that now covered the kitchen window. The lights had been on, Dylan had been looming over her. Whatever James had seen had made him leave, turn around and walk away.

"Oh God," she muttered. "This is terrible. What must he think?"

Brendon took a big slug of wine, the drink creating tiny pink crescents above his top lip on either side of his mouth. He set the wine down and shrugged.

"Brendon," Megan said, feeling the sting of tears again. "Tell me, what did he do, what did he say? Did he look mad?"

"He looked…"

"What?"

"Well it's hard to say, he was just standing there, holding a bottle of champagne by the looks of it, but I was in rather a rush, darling, I'd just nearly taken out an old dear walking a poodle and a jogger with a flashing hat."

"Champagne." He'd brought champagne. He always spoilt her. Champagne was becoming a habit, one she could get used to.

Or could have, because it sounded like he'd just gone, vanished.

How could he?

"He didn't say anything, though," Brendon went on, stroking Gucci who was now sitting by his feet. "He was just staring through the window at…well, whatever he could see."

"Damn. He'll have seen me and Dylan, likely Dylan half undressed, prat, and trying to kiss me. Oh, God, this is awful."

"Well that's what I saw. In fact anyone walking on by could have seen the whole spectacle."

"And just when we'd worked things out," Megan said, shaking her head. "I'd apologised for running out on him the other morning, he was coming round for…dinner but I had no idea what time and how typical it was the exact moment…"

"Dinner and…?"

"Brendon…" She sighed. "Oh what does it matter anyway? He's obviously gone. How could this be so messed up?"

She had a sudden urge to check and went to the window. She pulled the curtain aside and glanced out. The path was empty, the usual row of parked cars and an empty space beneath a street lamp a little way to the right. She spotted a jogger running past with a flashing red head torch.

"God, this is such a nightmare," she said, casting her gaze over the lawn then peering into the shadows. She hoped Dylan wasn't lurking in the dark, watching her, waiting for her. Willing her to slip up again and leave the door open, a window ajar. Biding his time till she stepped out of the house, which she'd have to at some point. She couldn't stay in forever.

She shuddered. How could they have been so close, so intimate and all set to spend their lives together then have the relationship turned upside down so quickly? Everything about it filled her with regret and, if she was honest now, fear.

A memory of the shadowy alcoves near her office flooded back to her. Had that been Dylan? Had he loitered in the dark corners waiting to get a glimpse of her, maybe speak to her, or worse?

A lump of nausea twisted her guts.

She snapped the curtain back into place and drew her fingers along it to make sure it was absolutely shut, not a crack of light escaping.

Dylan wouldn't do that surely. He had better things to do like going to the gym, getting legless with his mates, getting stupid tattoos.

But what if…?

She turned back to Brendon and pulled in a deep breath.

"You okay, sweetpea?" He looked concerned.

"Yes." She nodded, a little over enthusiastically. "Yes. I need to sort this out. I can't just let James leave like that, we had something…special, I'm sure of it." She puffed up her chest.

"Oh, good, your fighting spirit has returned." He grinned then knocked back more wine. "Good stuff this."

"Yes. It is." Megan strode to the table and took a gulp of her wine too. "Right," she said, then licked her lips. "Damage control." She glanced around.

"Oh, oh, I remember now," Brendon said, bouncing a little on the sofa and rubbing his hands together. "Hot Guy did say something…"

"What? What did he say?" Megan held her palms out. How could Brendon have neglected to tell her this?

"He said, sorry, you know, sorry, go ahead, or something like that to me and Gucci as we ran past him. I only just heard, we were going so fast, speed of sound and all that."

"Oh, is that it?" She was disappointed. "He just said sorry."

"Yes, sorry." He shrugged. "Well, I thought you should know."

"Thanks. I think." She patted her pocket then glanced at the table and the island. "Where's my phone?"

"How would I know?" Brendon looked around.

"I need to call James."

"And say what?"

"Explain. Explain that what he saw wasn't what he saw." She spotted a hairband on the table and reached for it, then pulled her hair back into a ponytail and secured it on the top of her head. She felt hot and bothered and her scalp still tingled a little as if it remembered Dylan tugging at her hair.

"That sounds like it will do the trick," Brendon said, pulling down the edges of his mouth. "What he saw wasn't what he saw."

"Well you know, tell him that Dylan hadn't been invited, that I didn't want him here in my home." She looked over at the kettle, wondering if her phone was there. No, maybe it was in her purse. "If I can just explain, he'll understand. He's not a like Dylan, he's not so full of himself that he can't see someone else's point of view. In fact that's his job, showing conflict from all perspectives and giving a balanced view."

"Very commendable." Brendon scooped Gucci up and set him on his lap. "What are you doing?"

"I'm looking for my phone." She scratched her head. "Where on Earth is it?"

"When did you use it last?"

"I…er…to text you. To come over."

"Well, is it in your pocket?"

She patted her jeans. "No."

"Hang on. I'll ring it." Brendon reached for his phone and unlocked the screen.

Within a few minutes her ring tone rang faintly in the distance.

"I can hear it," Brendon said, frowning. "Is it in your bedroom?"

"No." Megan looked towards the kitchen. She took a step closer. The singing was coming from the fridge. "Oh, bloody hell, I remember now." She pulled open the door and the music got louder.

Her phone was sitting next to a couple of bottles of Stella and a lump of cheese.

"What on earth is it doing in there?" Brendon asked, shaking his head.

Megan huffed as she retrieved the phone. The case was cold. "I didn't want to risk Dylan seeing that I'd texted you so I hid it in here after I sent the message."

"Good idea." He sat back and crossed his legs. "So do you have Hot Guy's number?"

"James, his name is James." She flicked through her contacts until she found his details. "And yes, I have, so this will all be sorted out in a jiffy."

"Absolutely." Brendon nodded confidently. "I'm sure he'll be relieved to hear from you. He really did look quite shocked."

"Did he?" Her belly tightened at the thought of what James had seen and what must have gone through his mind. The scene must have looked pretty damning. But it was an optical illusion—what he'd witnessed wasn't true. She just had to tell him that.

But that would mean confessing to the wedding, running from the altar. He already knew she was a runner.

Maybe she'd keep that bit of history to herself. Yes, she'd tell him another time. When she knew him better, when she'd managed to stick around for a few dates without getting the urge to flee and acting on it.

She'd just say he was an ex who was taking a while to get the hint that they were over. Once she explained that there was nothing between them, that the affection was one-sided, James would understand, she was sure of it.

She hit call and pressed the cool surface of the phone to her ear.

Brendon watched on expectantly, clearly loving the drama now the threat of getting a punched nose was over.

She heard the familiar ringing and paced to the right. It continued and she spun, strode to the left.

"Answer," she whispered. "Come on, answer, James."

The more it rang the tenser she became.

Eventually it went to voicemail.

"You've reached James Carter, I'll get back to you when I can."

Straight to the point, his voice still sent a shiver of longing through her. But should she leave a message? Try to explain the situation?

She looked at Brendon. "It's gone to voicemail."

"Oh, dear God, hang up." He flapped his hands. "Hang up. Hang up."

She quickly did as instructed. "Why? I could maybe leave a—"

"Are you crazy? You can't say something like this in a message. You need to speak to him. Face to face would be ideal but at the very least an actual conversation on the phone." He shook his head. "Goodness only knows what you'd say…"

"I'd just tell him that Dylan was an ex, that he hadn't been invited round but just turned up. Then things got a bit heated—"

"See stop right there."

"What?"

"Heated. That's the wrong word entirely, because things did look heated from out there." He pointed at the window. "And James won't listen beyond that. You need to say Dylan wouldn't take no for an answer. That he's obsessed with you. Keeps begging you to go back to him, proposing and all that."

"You really think I should mention the proposal?"

"Mmm, maybe not. That was loopy." Brendon spun his finger by his ear. "No one wants to think they're getting involved with a woman who has a loopy ex-boyfriend. Mega hassle."

Megan stared at the phone. Brendon was right. Dylan was mega hassle. He was also her baggage, and a stalker, or so it seemed.

But perhaps he'd taken the hint now. Maybe she wouldn't hear from Dylan anymore. She couldn't have been any clearer that they were over.

"Try Hot Guy, I mean James again." Brendon nodded at the phone as he tickled Gucci's chin. "He'll probably answer now. But word it carefully. Tell him Dylan is out of your life now but it took that crunch moment to make it happen." He paused and waggled his perfectly arched eyebrows. "Tell him to come round and you'll show him just how sorry you are that he had to see the whole thing."

The thought of making up with James was very appealing. "Good idea," she said, hitting redial.

Again she listened to the ringing. Each time she heard the sound, her heart sank. He wasn't going to pick up.

She shook her head when it went to message and ended the call.

"Seems he doesn't want to talk to me."

"Give him a while, he's probably driving." Brendon patted the sofa. "Come and sit here."

Megan snuggled against him, glad that she had Brendon there with her. If she didn't have him she'd go to pieces.

"I'll try him again later. It takes about twenty minutes to get from his place to here."

"There you go, that's all it is." Brendon rubbed her shoulder. "Try again in twenty minutes, have a chat and all will be right as rain."

Megan sighed. She certainly hoped so, because right now, it felt as though her world was crashing down, which was a crying shame because only an hour ago it had all been so bright and exciting.

Damn Dylan and his thick head, stubbornness and delusions that she'd ever consider taking him back. He'd gone and ruined everything.

18

Megan tried to call James seven more times over the course of the evening but there was never any answer. Just his message service.

She heeded Brendon's advice—even after he'd gone home and she pressed the phone to her ear one last time, listened to the ringing then James' deep voice—and didn't leave a message.

Eventually she went to bed, exhausted not just from a busy day but also from an emotionally wrought evening.

She'd just pulled off her clothes and slipped into bed when an idea came to her. Should she go to his house? It wouldn't take long to get dressed again, jump in a cab and get there. Then she could explain everything, smooth it over, make it okay.

She sat and stared at a photograph she had on the wall of her parents and Olivia. Damn, she missed them. Missed having her mum to talk to, her sister to take her mind off adult things and just have fun with. Her dad gave pretty good hugs too, even if he didn't know what was upsetting her, he still hugged generously and unconditionally.

Why were they so far away? Of course she knew the answers but they were of little comfort.

A tear welled and she blinked hoping it would reabsorb—it didn't. Instead it trickled down her cheek. She flopped back onto the pillow and let it soak into the soft cotton. A quiet sob bubbled up from her chest and she bunched her hands beneath her chin, drew her knees up and wished it would all go away—all this damn mess with Dylan. She couldn't go to James' house. It was too late. Everything was ruined.

Sleep was slow to arrive and when it did, her dreams were laced with thoughts of James, Dylan and dark figures lurking in shadows. Her heart beat fast and sweat prickled over her skin. Dylan's crazed eyes haunted her. James was there but fading, his outline drifting away, swallowed by fog and erased from her sight. She was losing him. He was lost. Gone.

Eventually morning came but Megan felt no less tired. Frantic dreams and vivid memories had robbed her of rest. The first thing she did was check her phone. Maybe James had called in the night and she hadn't heard it ring. Perhaps he'd left a text message, saying he'd see her today.

Nothing. Not even a good morning from Brendon. But then it was only six a.m., too early for him to be up and about.

She showered, dressed and made a pot of tea. She'd get to the office early and make a start on the last fashion slot for *Ralph and Jayne*. Then leave a list of daily and weekly jobs she'd need Enid to keep on top of while she went into design mode and worked on next season's collection. She'd likely do that from home, where she would be less distracted.

Enid was a keeper for sure. A bunch of flowers for Georgie to say thank you for sending such a competent assistant was in order. It was what had put her off getting help for so long, the thought of having someone scatty disturbing her ordered system. And yes, she would admit it now, as James had pointed out, giving up control was indeed hard when Winter Shoes was so important to her.

James.

Just thinking of him again made her heart ache.

It was the lack of anything, no communication at all, that hurt. If she'd hoped that Brendon had been wrong and it wasn't James that he'd dodged on the path, that hope was dashed now. James hadn't come to see her as organised, hadn't called to say why not or even texted an excuse. No, he thought she was with another man, and she had no way of telling her side of the story if he wouldn't even give her a chance.

She grabbed her handbag and slipped into a pair of espadrilles then scooped up her phone. She paused and looked at it. There had to be something she could do. In fact there was, she'd message him, then he'd have to see her reasoning. She thought for a moment then…

James. I'm sorry not to have seen you last night and I think I know why. But please, let me explain. It isn't what you think. Can we meet at Frank's later? Megan x

She hit send. Her mouth was dry and her heart beat wildly. Brendon would likely have lots to say about that rash course of action but tough, she had to do something, passive misery wasn't her style.

She went to the front door. Another envelope with just her name on it had been slotted through the letterbox. A rush of dread went through her. Had Dylan been back to her flat, in the night, while she'd slept? The thought made her feel sick.

With shaky hands she opened it. This time, as she unfolded the A4 piece of paper she could see it wasn't blank. Her focus blurred slightly as she read it.

You are the love of my life.
I will have you in my life.
I will get you back.
Soon.

"Oh God." It was him—Dylan. And still crazed by the sound of it.

She stared at the shut door. Was he out there? Waiting?

She had no idea, but equally she refused to be intimidated by him. She was tougher than that. He was just being an idiot.

Megan braced herself then opened the front door.

Nothing, no one.

She let out a sigh of relief, walked outside and breathed deeply. London fumes took the edge off a summer's morning as did an anonymous letter. She frowned and strode towards the Tube station. An irritated knot formed in her stomach that not even the birds singing in a lone cherry tree could ease.

As she walked into her office, all quiet because the estate agents were still an hour off arriving, her phone rang. She scrabbled for it then plucked it from her purse.

"Hello."

Nothing.

She glanced at the screen. Caller ID withheld.

"Hello, is that you?" she asked. Was it James? God, she hoped so.

Still nothing. Though wait, she *could* hear something. It sounded like traffic in the distance.

She held the phone closer, straining to hear. Yes, it was, the faint rumble of a road.

Damn it.

"Dylan, is that you?"

The phone went dead.

"You… It *is* you!" All those mysterious calls she'd been having. The ones that made the hairs on the back of her neck tingle and her guts roll. It had been him all along. Pestering her, hassling her, wanting to wind her up. She should have guessed.

Placing the phone on her desk, she stared at it. What should she do? Change her number? No, because what if James called, or her parents, or Georgie or Brendon? It would never work, besides, all her business contacts had that number, it was too important to give up because of Dylan.

"Bloody hell, Dylan. Why don't you just let it go?" She paced to the window and looked across the street at Frank's. The sun was spreading light over the cobbles and created a slash of gold over its usually dark windows and door. She longed to see James walking towards the bar the way he always did. Big purposeful strides, head bent if the weather was cool, hands shoved in his pockets and leather shoes beating the cobbles.

Her phone rang again from the desk.

Caller ID withheld.

She hit answer. "Dylan, stop hassling me."

"Did you get my love letter?"

"Love letter! Creepy letter more like. Give it a rest."

"But I need to see you, honeypie." There was a steeliness to his tone. "You can't ignore my letters and calls."

So it *was* all him. He'd given his sick game away now. "No. What's the point?"

"I've lost everything," he said. "I need you back, and I'm sorry about last night, really I am. I got emotional, carried away. You know you've always made me lose my mind when we start getting physical, you're just so damn irresistible."

Megan sighed and walked back to the window. A sparrow landed in one of the topiary trees outside Frank's and pecked at the leaves. "I've said everything I have to say to you, Dylan."

"But I have so much more to say to you, Megan. Please, don't throw this all away. We have such a bright future."

"What don't you get?" She could feel her temper rising. "I don't want to be with you. I've moved on, you need to as well. Find a new girlfriend, make a new future with someone else."

"But I want you." His voice was whiney.

"But you can't have me."

"Yes I can."

She heard an intake of air, like he was breathing deep.

"And," he went on, "I will have you."

"Oh God!" She stepped backwards.

A large, dark figure had appeared at her window. Shock made her giddy for a second then she saw who it was.

Dylan.

He was there—on the other side of the glass. And he was staring at her with his mad eyes. His shoulders were so wide and menacing.

"What the hell?" she said, gripping the edge of the desk and keeping the phone pressed to her ear.

"Let me in." He nodded at the luckily locked door. It was weird to hear him in her ear and faintly through the glass, seeing his lips move.

"No, no I won't, and why…why are you here?"

"To see you."

"Bloody hell. How long have you been out there?" No wonder she'd heard traffic, it was the road at the end of Change Street.

"A while, but, Megan, for you I'll wait for as long as it takes."

"You're mad."

"Not mad." He paused and patted his hand over his T-shirt, flattening it against where she knew his tattoo to be. "I'm just in love, and being in love makes me very determined. My broken heart needs mending, and you're the only one who can do that."

A kernel of fear grew within her. She'd never get away from this. She couldn't have been more blunt the night before, yet here he was, lurking outside her flat and her office, waiting for her. What was the matter with him? And had he done it before, this waiting around for her?

She recalled that night she'd first had a drink with James. How freaked out she'd been just crossing the cobbles to the bar because she'd felt sure someone was watching her from the darkest of the shadows.

Dylan?

She'd bet her last stiletto that it had been him.

She stared at him, anger and nerves tangling her emotions. She'd never get away from his craziness. He was messing with her head the way he always had. Trying to control her. Well, she wouldn't let him, not this time. It seemed he'd already destroyed her fledgling relationship with James—the first decent man she'd met in a long time—but she wouldn't let him destroy her newfound confidence and sense of self. "You have to leave."

"Or what, you'll call Brendon again? Like I'm really scared of him." He shook his head and sneered.

"No, the police. This is harassment, Dylan. There are laws to stop people like you doing this kind of thing."

"I'm your fiancé, Megan, what will they say? I'm entitled to be with you."

"No you're not! We're over. I sent you the ring back." She shook her bare finger at him through the glass. "Now fuck off."

"Not until you agree to meet me, later."

"No. No way." *Really?*

"Then I'm not going anywhere."

She sighed and rubbed her fingers over her forehead. There was only one thing for it. She'd have to do it. "Okay, where?"

"There." He jabbed his thumb over his shoulder. "That bar opposite."

Not a chance in hell. "Okay." She nodded. "What time?"

"Seven."

"Yes. I'll see you then." Lying didn't usually come easy to Megan but these were exceptional circumstances, not to mention self-preservation. "Seven. We'll talk more then."

He grinned. Obviously chalking it up as a victory and a step closer to winning her back. "Be there, or I'll come looking for you."

"I'll see you later, Dylan. But right now I've got work to do." She pointed at her desk. "Goodbye." She didn't wait for him to reply, just clicked her phone off.

He lowered his from his ear then blew her a kiss.

As quickly as he'd appeared he vanished. The light streamed once again into her office the moment his big bulk moved from view.

Sitting heavily on her chair, she hugged her arms around herself. What a bloody disastrous situation. And could it be any more unnerving? Dylan had been stalking her for the last couple of weeks. Making her doubt her sanity and putting her on edge. She'd almost thought she was imagining things yet all along he'd been tailing her.

If she could transport herself a million miles away, right this minute she would. She'd jump on a boat, a plane…a rocket if necessary. She was living a nightmare. One man she didn't want hounding her, and one man she did want so desperately her bones ached, ignoring her.

Or was he?

She quickly unlocked her iPhone and scrolled to messages. James had an iPhone too, she'd be able to see if he'd read her text.

She scanned the tiny writing beneath her words.

Yes.

He'd read it a few minutes ago.

But there was no reply.

Well probably he'd answer soon, then she'd be able to tell him everything. Well, not everything, but certainly explain who Dylan was.

She set the phone aside and stood. Put the kettle on then waved at one of the estate agents who walked past her window and looked in.

He was early, but she was glad. It made her feel less isolated. Dylan could still be hanging about.

How long was she going to have to cope with this? Maybe if she and James could work things out, Dylan would see her with a new boyfriend—she smiled a little at the thought of calling him that—and he'd give up the ghost of them. Stop hounding her to get back with him. The words on the note he'd put through her door in the night played on her mind.

You are the love of my life. I will have you in my life. I will get you back. Soon.

What did he mean? What lengths was he prepared to go to? And what did *soon* mean?

She poured herself a green tea which always calmed her then went back to her desk, praying that she'd see a return message from James.

Nothing.

There was only one thing for it. She'd call him.

She did just that, strutting the width of the room and back as it rang.

Voicemail.

"For crying out loud." She dropped her phone onto her desk, rougher than she'd intended but luckily it survived. "What is the matter with men?"

"Megan, Megan, are you in there?"

A sharp knock at the door made Megan's heart trip. But it was a woman's voice. Enid.

"Yes, hang on." Quickly she opened the door.

Enid shuffled in, loaded down with what appeared to be a large shopping bag. "I thought I'd come in early, sort through that design filing cabinet. I've brought some dividers and spacers, get it all alphabetical and neat."

Megan stuck her head out of the door, glanced left and right—no one in sight—then shut it again, flicking the lock too.

She was sure she'd never forget to secure a door again. She'd likely always be bracing herself to step outside too, in case Dylan was there.

"You okay, dear?" Enid asked, placing the bags near the second desk.

"Yes, fine." *Far from it.* "But I might be going away for a while." *Am I?* Yes. She was. She needed to.

Dylan had pushed her too far. She felt hunted, hounded, how the hell would she concentrate on the new designs she had stacking up in her imagination?

Plus James' lack of communication had worn down her already fragile confidence and trust in men.

It was time to take a break.

Far away.

Didn't matter where.

She just had to get out of there.

Her legs twitched at the thought. Excitement pounded through her.

"Oh, where are you going?" Enid looked surprised.

"Abroad, to the sun." She hoped. But in all honesty, it didn't matter. She'd take an igloo at the moment as long as it was away from London. "Do you think you'll be able to manage without me? I know you haven't been here long but…"

"Well yes, I'm sure it will all be fine. And you'll be at the end of the phone if I need you, won't you, dear?"

"Absolutely, of course." She nodded and grabbed her phone. She held it up and smiled, hoping to instil confidence in the one person Winter Shoes needed most at the moment. Because the way her brain was, she was fried.

"That's okay then." Enid smiled in a motherly way. "You take your time, I've got plenty to be getting on with and those suppliers need chasing up, as do those high street orders."

Damn she'd forgotten about them. "Yes, yes of course."

"But it's on my to-do list." She tapped a bit of paper on the table. "So it will get done, if it's on the list, it always gets done."

"And cancel my last appearance on the *Ralph and Jayne* show. I'm not doing it." Was she really saying that? Yes, she had to prioritise her sanity at this point in time. There'd be other opportunities, she'd make sure of it. Bigger ones, more glamorous ones, she knew what she wanted and she'd go out and get it.

"Consider it done. Now you take care." Enid smiled kindly and without any judgment about the sudden decisions.

"Thank you." Megan grabbed her bag. "I mean it, thank you so much. I'll call, later, or tomorrow. And, Enid…I'm so glad you're here. Really I am, I can't say how much…" If she'd known the older woman better she'd have hugged her, but she was all off kilter and didn't want to freak out her one and only employee any more than she probably was.

"Go, it's fine. I've got it." Enid smiled, sat then pushed at the sleeves on her powder-blue cardigan. "And take care."

Megan didn't need telling twice. She practically ran from the office, leaving the keys in the door so Enid could come and go as she pleased. She'd give her a raise for this.

There were a few people milling about and she dashed past them to the main street hoping she wouldn't suddenly hear Dylan's footsteps behind her or him calling her name.

She didn't.

Her head was now spinning with possibilities. Where should she go? What should she do?

She'd watched a film once about a man who just turned up at the airport and demanded a ticket for the first flight out of Paris. He'd had enough of his life and it was his way of letting fate take control.

That's what she'd do.

She'd go to Heathrow and buy the first available seat out of the UK. It could be Brazil, Cairo, Sydney – didn't matter so long as she wasn't in London.

She flagged a cab, unable to face the Tube, and headed for home. She pulled her phone out once more.

"Last chance, James."

Nothing.

She dialled Georgie who answered on the third ring. "Hey you, what's up?"

"Everything, Georgie, I'm out of here."

"What?" There was shock in her best friend's voice. "Why? What's happened?"

"Nothing and everything. I can't stay in London. I need a break. A bit of me time. Enid is awesome, I have every faith in her, so I'm going to duck out of living for a while."

"Duck out of living. What the hell are you talking about?"

Megan sighed. "Dylan."

"What about Dylan?"

"He was round again, last night and this morning. He's in a bad way, a sad way. He's messed it up big time between me and James and to be honest, he's making it hard to get my life back on track."

"Why? What happened?"

"I'll tell you later. I'll call when I get there."

"Where? Get where?"

"I don't know yet." Megan felt bad for worrying Georgie like this. She could hear the alarm in her friend's voice.

"Why don't you know? Bloody hell, Megan, you're scaring me. What's going on?"

"I'm fine. I promise. But I'm in a rush. I need to get away for a bit. I'll explain everything later. Bye."

"Don't go."

"I have to."

"Okay, okay, but call me back sooner than when you…get there, wherever *there* is."

"I will. From the airport okay."

"Airport…"

"I love you. I'll make it up to you."

"I love you too, and if it's what you need to do then I'm behind you, one hundred percent, but be careful and stay in touch, okay."

"I will, I promise. Bye for now."

She hung up and instantly dialled Brendon's number.

"I was just about to call you," he said. "How did you sleep?"

"Not well. And I've seen Dylan again. He was hanging about near the office when I went in at seven."

"What?" He gasped. "We need to get the police involved. This is serious."

"He won't listen to them. He won't listen to anyone. He's obsessed, Brendon."

"He'll have to."

"Well yes, maybe. But for now I'm off."

Silence.

"I'm off," she said again.

"Where?" Unlike Georgie his voice was low and calm.

"I don't know. I'm going to head to Heathrow and get the first flight out that has a spare seat."

"That's crazy talk."

"Well maybe that's what Dylan and James have done to me, sent me round the bloody bend."

"No, I'll tell you what they've done, they've made you put on your running shoes."

Running shoes?

Brendon was right. That's exactly what she was doing, she was running. Something she'd got pretty damn good at of late. But what the hell. Running suited her down to the ground. Running felt good, better than anything else she could think of doing.

"And what about *Ralph and Jayne,* you have one more appearance with them."

"It's cancelled."

"What?"

"That's just the way it is. I'm sorry I really am grateful but... Listen, I have to go. I've told Georgie I'm off for a bit, but I didn't have time to fill her in on the details. Tell her if you get to her first, if not I'll call her from..."

"From wherever on the planet you end up."

"Yes."

"Let's hope it's not Kabul then, not sure how good mobile signal is from there."

"I'll be sensible."

"Why don't I believe you?" He paused. "Love ya, take care."

"Love you too. Give Gucci a pat from me."

Two hours later Megan walked through the doors of Heathrow airport. The atmosphere was buzzing. Passengers filtering through the system, suitcases rattling on their wheels, kids running around excitedly.

She paused and looked up at the departure board. She had one large roll along case with her that she'd thrown an assortment of clothes and shoes into that would be suitable for beaches, rain-soaked cities and warm green hills.

Vancouver. Amsterdam. Dubai. Cape Town. Paris. Karachi. New York. Reykjavik. Istanbul. Her gaze settled on Istanbul. Maybe that was her fate? A land of sweet spices, exotic scents, vibrant colours. She inhaled deeply, almost smelling the busy markets, and paced towards the British Airways desk.

She queued for a few minutes at the ticket desk, half listening to a family who were chatting excitedly about Mickey Mouse and magic castles.

What would she do if James rang when she was about to board? Would she go back? Change her plans?

No. Sod it. She was getting away from it all. She needed a holiday.

Eventually it was her turn and she walked up to the desk. "Hi."

"Hello. Welcome to British Airways." A young girl with shiny orange lipstick welcomed her. "What can I do for you?"

"I need a ticket?"

"Of course. Where to?"

"Anywhere."

"Anywhere?" Her eyebrows raised and she tipped her head to the side.

"Yes, anywhere. I've got to get away, for a holiday you know?"

"Indeed." A smiled spread on her face. "How exciting. I've always wanted someone to ask for a ticket to anywhere. So romantic, but also exciting and mysterious."

"Well it would be more so if I wasn't going on my own," Megan said with a shrug. But even so she smiled. It *was* exciting now that she was doing it, she couldn't deny that, but also scary too.

"Let me see." The woman stared at her screen, her long lashes fluttering. "The next flight…with seats." She paused. "Economy or business?"

"Economy is fine."

"Well in that case." She grinned.

Megan held her breath. What would fate throw at her? Where would she be waking up tomorrow? What continent would she walk on? What language would she hear?

"Where?" Megan asked. "Where is it to, the ticket?"

"I think you're going to like it. The land of dreams, where stars are made, the place anything can happen if you want it to desperately enough."

Megan rolled her hand in the air. "Which is…?"

"I hope you've packed your bikini and your best beach shoes. You, lucky thing, are off to sunny California, Los Angeles to be precise!"

The third in the best-selling
In Other Words series

She planned everything…except him.

Part of the best-selling
What's her Secret? imprint

She wanted him. Her sister married him.

The third in the hilarious
Samantha Lytton series

Unforgettable. That's what she's not.

The first volume in the engaging
Seasoned Women series

Part of the best-selling
What's her Secret? imprint

A past she wants to forget…

TOTALLY
BOUND
Home of Erotic Romance